BRAVÍA

ROBERT A. MUSTELL

BRAVÍA

a selection of short stories

ANDREA AMOSON

REDACTELIER
BOOKS

Contents

First Printing, 2024
Redactelier Books
Dallas, Texas, U.S.A.

For Kristof Jerry, for your migratory soul, for your strong little hands, for your musical laughter.

For Ignatio Enrique, for your millennial soul, for your leaps of joy, for your green-coffee eyes.

Out of Laurides

Selection of short stories from "Érase una vez Laurides"
(Once upon a time Laurides)

I

The Scrivener

Tania had a coquettish name, a good facade to hide the voluminous body she had gained by eating two milanesas a day. She wasn't Argentine, but once, in some hallway of her house, she heard that her grandmother was born beyond the Andes, had hair as caramel-colored as fresh honey, and a pair of green eyes her grandfather couldn't resist. That's why Tania made milanesas once a week, on Sundays, to be exact, after attending her crochet and cross-stitch meetings. True, because maybe her greatest extravagance was pretending to be Argentine, even if it was in the secrecy of her frying pans.

She didn't tell anyone she loved Ricarte either, the once vigorous reporter who had arrived a decade ago to work at the newspaper, unfortunately illiterate, but with such a prodigious memory that he could report the information and write it in his head on the way to the office to meet Tania, who acted as a scrivener, typing everything Ricarte dictated.

Ricarte's youth had faded gracefully, though not to Tania, who, seeing him appear every morning ten years later, ignored that he dragged his feet as if he carried the weight of all the news stored in his talented head. It seemed like yesterday when she saw him show up in the newsroom, athletic and white arms, a half-buttoned shirt, and a tuft of curly hair escaping from his chest. Ricarte, in his forties, was an agile man who had nothing to envy the young men of the city. Tania had seen him grow in moral height, watching him silently endure the insults of his three colleagues, who swore he had come to take their jobs, so highly recommended had he arrived from the capital, to the respect he earned by harvesting more than two hundred front-page news stories. Ricarte had beaten the competition journalistically, with his last-minute, truthful, and precise information, to Tania's devotion, who hadn't noticed when Ricarte began to gain a belly; his chest hair straightened and turned white until it disappeared completely, moving to a short but rebellious tuft at the base of his ears.

Tania, on the other hand, seemed preserved in formaldehyde, as if she had been born old and rounded. She was the only daughter of Doña Dominga, the famous owner of a greengrocer's that could offer Pica lemons in all seasons, and had inherited from her Argentine mother one green eye, just one, while the other was dark brown. For years, Doña Dominga tried to hide her different irises behind her escarole lettuces, and for years, Tania wished to have something as spectacular as a pair of striking eyes. However, as we've said, the only striking thing Tania had was her name, which she heard her father had heard, in turn, at the great Romanini circus that stopped in the city before she was born—an emergency stop because the ship, whose original destination was Valparaiso, had broken down, and they had to dock on the Lauridense coast. The city's streets turned into an eternal carnival, as the old newspaper reporters told, with sword swallowers, stilt walkers, and jugglers roaming the main avenue out of sheer boredom, trying to kill time. After several pleas from the mayor, the head circus performer agreed to disembark the tent and give a show. They say the most glorious committee of beings the sleepy city had ever witnessed disembarked: a giraffe, a famished lion, a pair of macaws with colors so vivid, so red, calypso, and turquoise that it hurt to look at them, plus some artists from Peru, Ecuador, Colombia, and the main attraction: the glamorous Ilinov Brothers.

From the first show, with a full tent, Tania's father fell in love with Tanya Ilinova, the younger sister of the trapeze artists, the one who climbed Mirko's back to get on the swing in mid-flight; who was thrown between Branko and Jelko's arms like a testimony; who appeared in the closing parade wearing a very short skirt and a top of a color quite similar to pink but so sharp and bright that no one could name it because such a tone had never been seen before in Laurides. The days passed with an infatuated man guarding the beautiful Tanya Ilinova at the port, a besotted man who couldn't conquer the girl but convinced her to come home, offering the personalized attention of his wife, a bed anchored to the floor with a window and door, and not the cabin she had to share with her brothers in the greasy belly of the ship. Tanya Ilinova accepted the offer, and it was Mirko, Branko, and Jelko who escorted her, not without first inspecting the house, the bedroom, and ensuring that there was indeed a wife who would protect the precarious honor of the circus artist. Doña Dominga accepted the affair as one accepted the husband's will in those times, without a word. Tania was born older than expected, though, as the untimely romance overshadowed the happy news that she was finally pregnant after over a decade of marriage.

The great circus performer continued offering night shows, but he had to suspend them when only four paupers showed up in the tent, Tania's father being one of them. The situation worsened when he left quickly, as soon as the Ilinov Act ended.

And so, very soon, Tanya Ilinova grew tired of the rocky path she had to cross to go to the bathroom, at the back of the house, the smell of dung coming from the neighboring pigeon coops that scented the Lauridense morning like a cloud of putrid birds, the night shows with an audience that neither paid nor applauded, except for one, and we know who that was, as if the sea air started to close Tanya Ilinova's throat little by little, leaving as the only solution to breathe the wooded vapors of the Belarusian forest. The Lauridenses were curious, envious, and amused as she dragged her load back to the ship one Monday morning after getting up determinedly and packing all of her belongings, taking her wheeled trunk, and crossing the five streets that separated the house from the port. A couple of weeks later, the Ilinovs left on another great ship bound for Guayaquil, leaving Tania's father heartbroken, but more than that, with unfulfilled dreams of caressing that elastic and fibrous body, those pointed breasts, those very long legs, as long as desire itself.

Doña Dominga then opened the bedroom the beautiful

usurper had occupied for three weeks, burned the sheets, the curtains, and the blanket, disinfected the floor and walls with bleach so vigorously that her fingers bled, and set out to prepare a small room for the future child, who would be born in two months and until then had no space in the house, which was all hallways, no rooms. The husband had destined that space, until the circus incident, for a carpentry workshop, but after the wrong move of giving it to the platonic lover, he had no choice but to leave it at his wife's disposal. The cleaning led to a fight, as the husband could no longer enter to smell the scent of sweaty jasmines that Tanya Ilinova had left in the room, and therefore, facing the imminent loss of everything, he demanded that Doña Dominga name the girl she was about to give birth to Tania. Doña Dominga didn't say a word, as was proper, but she prayed with a full heart to give birth to a boy, so she could call him Tanio and stigmatize him forever. She spent long nights imagining the humiliations Tanio would suffer because of the story of his name, and if it weren't for the revenge Doña Dominga imagined, in a grotesque act against her own blood, she wouldn't have endured the humiliation her husband had put her through. If the woman didn't rebel in public, rest assured that a storm was raging in her guts. She hoped Tanio would come into the world with swapped eyes too, she thought before sleeping, as if the word had become action. Thus, the months passed, the circus raised the tent, and the ship set sail. Then Tania was born, who was almost invisible and had brown eyes.

II

And with that desert gaze, Tania silently loved Ricarte. For a decade, she watched him come and go between the newsroom and his office, where she diligently cut out the photographs published in the newspaper each day to pair them with the original, placed both documents in a white envelope, wrote the headline of the news, the subject of the photograph, and the date with a blue pen, and then gave them a place in the files that surrounded her. A large room of files from floor to ceiling and wall to wall. Such had been her existence, with daily milanesas, dictations, and filing cabinets. A great existence, Tania reflected, considering that Doña Dominga, disappointed at having given birth to a girl, hadn't paid much attention to her, and, in summary, it had been her father who taught her to read, write, add, and subtract and finally accompanied her to the newspaper to ask for the job that Doña Panchita had abruptly left available after a sudden heart attack.

And when Tania turned thirty—that is, when her singleness was sealed—she went to the bank and withdrew all her money to rent a small apartment in order to escape her mother's constant vigilance. "Everything is fine," she thought, since we get used to our routines and shortcomings, until the last Sunday morning, when she was combing her straight hair in front of the mirror and discovered a green freckle in her right iris. The sight terrified her; she was already used to her invisibility, so why was she suddenly assaulted by something so distinctive? What terror she felt that Sunday morning upon seeing that freckle! How would her life change because of that oceanic spot that murmured beneath her pupil? Would it keep growing? It would be best not to think about it, she decided. However, by Monday, the freckle had grown. By Tuesday, it had taken on the appearance of a tear and was occupying the lower portion of her iris. By Wednesday, that emerald sea that lashed at the edge of her eyelashes had consumed her entire eye. She felt panic; she couldn't leave the house, showing the aberration that was now so evident. She searched her drawers for dark glasses, but she didn't own such luxuries—only some old copies of *Ecran* magazine she had stolen from the newspaper. She had the good idea to crochet a pirate patch with a sample of wool that had arrived at the store a few weeks ago, of a color similar to pink but much more intense—a color no one had ever seen and no one knew how to name.

With the eye patched, she left her small apartment, destined for the hospital, for the prolonged wait to receive medical attention. While waiting, she couldn't believe she had had the courage to show up at the newspaper the previous two days, days in which she stayed in her office, nervous, surrounded by newspapers and glue. The photographs from previous editions piled up on her desk without lifting her gaze, and when the three old reporters came to ask for the mayor's, the singer's, and the football player's portraits, she pointed to the file with her finger, pretending to be very busy cataloging images instead of getting up from her chair, as she used to do, promptly and diligently, as someone who doesn't eat milanesas, to attend to their requests. The hardest part of those days was Ricarte's entrance into the office, with his information overflowing in his head. As soon as he entered, he began dictating aloud, not even "Good morning, shall we begin?". Ricarte had become used to dictating to her as if she were a machine and not a woman with a pretty name and a voluptuous body capable of loving him as she did on new moon nights, swaying with his memory on the pillow, sweaty and panting.

As a result, Ricarte appeared on Monday and Tuesday, leaving Tania overcome with fear over the freckle in her eye. She also thought about this in the eternal queue at the hospital—about what it was that suddenly assaulted her, distinguished her, and made her different. And she remembered the three thousand two hundred days that Ricarte had ignored her precisely because she was so normal. She relived that first morning when Ricarte appeared at the newspaper asking for a job and they sent him to her office, where the only spare typewriter was, and where he confessed that he couldn't read or write, but with her help, he could get by and reach the top, just as he had done at the great capital newspaper, because he, he explained, had a daguerreotypic memory. That was the beginning of a relationship that never went beyond being professional and that soon ceased to be a relationship at all; she was nothing more than a functional Remington 520.

And how, with such phenomenal memory, had he not noticed that Tania had a spot growing in her right eye? How, for a decade, had he never thanked her? How, for a decade, had he entered and left her archive room as if she didn't exist, because, horror!, he put his beautiful, skillful hands into the drawers himself, without needing her help, and how many times had she fantasized about those same soft hands caressing her as if she were a photograph? But the only thing she had received was a monotonous dictation, coming from a fleshy, juicy, desired mouth and a gaze lost in the office ceiling.

The horror of the spot suddenly wounded her insides, suddenly turned into fire, and suddenly burned her in the crotch. The horror of the spot consumed her voraciously, turning her all green, all ocean, and all rage. And so, while Tania had been waiting for two hours to be seen at the hospital, she decided to get rid of Ricarte. Although the method was unclear, a resolution was reached.

III

The following Sunday morning, Doña Dominga had just prepared the dough to make the weekly milanesas when Tania left the bathroom, wearing a long skirt and white blouse with black stripes, ready for mass and her afternoon crochet meeting. She didn't speak a word, as was proper, since Sundays had been silent for years, so Doña Dominga could dedicate herself to her devotions without distractions. They left the house at the same time, one carrying her purse, the other her grocery bags, and each took a different direction.

At church, Tania did everything possible to look less rounded, to lift her shoulders, and to hold in her belly, but it seemed like the only thing she achieved was losing half a lung because her heart was pounding. Thus, the service ended, and Tania, who never stopped feeling the pounding of her ribcage, decided not to go to her friends' meeting, to avoid questions, to avoid "feeling normal," and to go straight to her apartment to scrutinize her tired appearance. Half an hour later, she was in front of the mirror, re-straightening the soft strands of her hair, carefully combing her eyelashes, pulling her cheeks with two fingers to imitate a lost freshness, and finally, even with a bit of fear, peering into her own pupil. The green freckle had grown, moving from one side to the other, as if marking a new, healthier territory. It had become an intense color, as if in another week it would consume her dark brown eye. The weight of that gaze fell on her reflection and, as if it were a ballast, pulled her shoulders forward. Her reflection threw herself onto the bed, but she didn't have the courage to follow it, as if keeping her composure prevented her from falling into a bottomless pit. Then she sat in front of the window, legs crossed, the fallen hands on her lap, and her eyes glued to the black sky with an invisible face, just because.

IV

The streets were starting to fill up, the lauridenses were waking from their forced siestas, and Tania encountered people who tried not to look at her directly, commenting sideways about her eye. At the exit of a school, children formed a circle around her and sang, "Rain, rain, the old lady is in the cave," even though she was not old and couldn't make it rain. She reached her apartment only to find Pego, the newspaper photographer, on the landing. The editor had sent him to find out what had happened, where she was, and who would be helping Ricarte write the major news of the day. She sent a message back to the editor, saying she had gone to the hospital, been given the afternoon off, and someone else should help Ricarte.

Pego left grumbling that the editor was very bad-tempered and would surely yell at him, which was true. We've only known one kind newspaper editor, but he soon lost his job because he was labeled a "sissy" during the military era.

Tania went to the kitchen, thinking of taking advantage of the time to prepare milanesas. What did it matter that she had no grandmother or Argentine blood? She loved the taste of cheese, ham, and meat mixed together. When she was cracking the fifth egg, she heard someone knock on her door. "What does Pego want now?" she grumbled. Opening the door, she saw it was Ricarte, with the typewriter under his arm. He was smiling, lively, and youthful.

"What happened, Tanita? Why didn't you go? You know I can't live without you..."

Tania looked at him incredulously, holding the bowl of eggs, the green eye visible, and Ricarte's patience.

"What do you want?" she responded bluntly, barring his way.

"What do I want, silly? For you to help me, of course... I have a scoop; it involves Dr. Ponce, the hospital... I uncovered a scandal: the man receives all kinds of payments and even sleeps with Luchita; you know her? The old prostitute, even her false teeth, fall out. Will you help me?"

The typist looked at him intently.

"Why are you looking at me so insistently?" he asked, unaware of the different eyes.

"Nothing; come in; let's work."

They entered the living room. Ricarte sat at the table, installed the typewriter slowly, put paper in it, moved the chair, and theatrically cleaned it with his handkerchief.

"Everything is ready, my queen," he said, pointing to the chair.

Tania went to the kitchen to put down the egg mixture and wash her hands. On her return, she noticed that the scene Ricarte had created in her home was an exact replica of her office, only missing the floor-to-ceiling, wall-to-wall file cabinets. Tania, of the beautiful name and voluptuous body, sat down and began to type what Ricarte dictated. Thus, the reporter unraveled the news, launched accusations, spoke of morals and good customs, and said that certain things should never be transgressed.

Tania realized that the big scoop would mean the end of the good doctor, the free care, a life dedicated to a town that smelled of bird droppings and its people, so tough, so fierce, so poor.

"Done," Tania said sadly.

"Great, little queen! With this, I'll surely get a raise," Ricarte said, putting his hand in his pants pocket.

"But hurry up! The night shift has started; see if they'll let you include the news at the last minute."

"True! Look at the time... But it's Romero's shift; you know he hits the bottle; he's probably pickled in front of the press."

"Romero?" Tania asked, biting her lip a bit.

"Yes, Romero..."

"It'll work out; it really will. Hurry up, hurry up!"

Tania saw him off at the door of her little apartment. She watched him walk away, looked at his back, and, for the first time, noticed it was slumped. Where there were once straight shoulders, there was now a weak roundness. The once-firm and powerful buttocks of a decade ago were now just two flattened alfajores that didn't fill out his pants. His legs had bowed and thinned, and a monk's bald spot was appearing at the nape of his neck, but the worst were the bristly hairs sprouting from his ears.

"Goodbye, Ricarte," she murmured, closing the door.

She went to the bedroom. From under the pillow, she took out a photograph of what had been her love for years, a black-and-white rectangle showing him receiving the last journalistic award he had won. She wrote on the back, "Ricarte Obregón," and added the date, time, and title: unrequited love. Back in the living room, she looked for one of the white envelopes in her purse and put the photograph in it. She wandered around the little apartment, searching, and finding no filing cabinet and no better option, she put the envelope in the oven with the milanesas.

She lay down uncomfortably that day. But determined to do without Ricarte, she found one of the *Ecran* magazines, flipped through until she found the athletic and white arms, the half-buttoned shirt, and a tuft of curly hair escaping from Marlon Brando's chest, and let herself be loved by those arms that knew exactly how to caress her.

The next morning, with the patch off her eye, she went out to see how the bicolor world was and found it beautiful.

At the newspaper stand, her friend the newsagent greeted her with curiosity, perhaps because of her irises, but then with naturalness. Something else seemed to worry him.

"Tanita, how's it going?... What a mess Ricarte made, huh? Did you hear he got fired? And they might press charges."

"No! Poor Ricarte, what happened?" Tania replied without waiting for an answer, because she already knew.

She grabbed one of the copies, folded it, and tucked it under her arm. She walked away with a smooth and rhythmic step, with the headline still dancing in her green retina, the glorious headline she had written, the news she had twisted in Ricarte's ignorant eyes and published in the drunkenness of the night shift press manager, the big journalistic scoop highlighted on the front page of the main edition, exonerating the doctor and pointing the inquisition at himself, accusing Ricarte of extortion, influence peddling, and idiocy, dragging the editor into the wave of accusations.

The city's top reporter signed the article that was on the front page.

*****

Ecran: Ecran magazine was a renowned Chilean publication dedicated to the art of cinema, offering insightful reviews, features, and news about the film industry.

2

The Gulf at Dawn

The sea is a line, and at the end, the world finishes. The voice of the other shakes her. "The sea is our ally," he speaks like a soldier, "our ally." The voice of the other yells at her to hurry up; they have little time; you never know... never, he adds angrily. Drool hangs from his snout; another dog leads her; another bone. They get on the boat. Grab the oars. The sea is a line. The dog squeezes her arm and says, "Faster, more..." They need to reach the port before the sun hangs up there. "There is no line between the sea and the sky," Joaquina whispers. The dark blue finally begins to separate, and the ocean mirrors what is above. The sun rises in the east over the Gulf, the cotton clouds dyed yellow, the reflection of the stars, thousands of eyes closing over the water. "Faster, this is not a stroll!" the other barks. And Joaquina quickens her rowing and is glad to have strength. This time, she won't desert, cry, or moan. "Third time's the charm," she whispers.

Silence. Only the soft sound of wood caressing the water can be heard. The other knows the place; the stubborn soldier knows how to move; the memory of his expert sense of smell in these crossings once free, before the guards, the walls, the barbed wire.

In the sand, I wrote your name...

Joaquina loses the thread and doesn't remember how many days she's been walking. They left as twenty; now there are eight. The dog hurries her; the sea is not a line. She will tell her grandchildren about the crossing and how foolish she is; she's not even married. She will tell the grandchildren that the sea at night is a line, and at the dark and rumbling bottom, everything ends. She will say that Columbus was wrong and the earth is flat because every time you try to catch the curve to head north, you die and fall into the abyss full of monsters.

When the shore is in sight, the dog yells at them to run. The other urges her to dive into the water: "Quick! Hide!" The weight of her pants against the waves, the shoes sticking to the wet sand, her chest bursting from the effort and terror. Joaquina reaches the bushes, half-blind, and pushes into the thorny arms of the bushes. She feels the burning in her thighs, the denim tearing like rice paper. Thorns and blood. She doesn't stop running or thinking about what she will tell her grandchildren; it doesn't matter if she's not married.

In the sand, I wrote your name, and then I erased it...

She shakes her head to forget her father's favorite song.

She crosses the leafy wall, and at the end, a truck awaits them. They climb in hurriedly and are taken to a shed. Other mutts are in charge of the shed now that the dog has vanished. Quickly, wash up a bit. "For what?" Joaquina whispers, approaching the bucket of water. She cleans herself and checks her legs; the thorns stick out through the tears in her pants. She tries to remove them, but she can't. There is no more time. They must keep moving. They get into the truck, piled on top of each other on the floor. Three fall on top of her, and someone digs a knee into her back. She can't breathe, but she endures, knowing she can. She is very close; she will reach Houston and remove the thorns. She will return to her studies and take care of the elderly. To dream that someone dreams that she can stay. *In the sand, I wrote your name, and then I erased it.* The truck engine roars, the wheels skid, the piled bodies creak, hurt, cry. After a few bumps, the truck speeds away at dawn.

...so no one would step on your name, María Isabel.

3

What Glorita Has

We meet on an ordinary afternoon—as ordinary as an afternoon can be—in the waiting room of the city's best addiction psychiatrist. We're both broken, I think to myself as I watch her wearing a black jacket with red trim; it looks like a miner's jacket. She looks at me, and I wonder if she speaks my language. The language is a loss for me. My three children, my losses. My two husbands are my losses. She sits with her legs apart like an unstitched doll, but at the same time as if asking permission to exist; she doesn't look old or young. There isn't a single gray hair on her head, which strikes me as round, incredibly round, and perfectly round, as if it could roll and kick across the floor. I debate whether to talk to her or not; it is clear that she is waiting too. We are both a pair of women searching for some answer in life, either in the supermarket line or in the psychiatrist's waiting room.

"Granma?" As she comes from the doctor's office, a young girl interrupts her, smiling.

"Are you ready?" The woman responds in Spanish, and that encourages me; maybe we can talk.

"I need to go to the bathroom," says the young woman, turning around in the restroom direction. This path is very familiar to me because every time I have to wait, my bladder attacks, causing me to get up three or four times to go to the bathroom.

"Is she your daughter?" I finally dared to ask, regretting it instantly. If she called her grandma, how dumb am I?

She replies, "My granddaughter."

"Oh..." I realize she doesn't want to continue our conversation.

We both look at the ground as if there were a big TV screen where we could lose ourselves for a moment, not having to hold each other's gaze or smile forcibly. It would have been better if I hadn't spoken to her. I look at the clock; at any moment, Glorita, my goddaughter, will arrive, dragging those too-long legs she inherited from my *compadre* and the thick arms she got from my *comadre*. Gloria, Glorita, is the closest thing I have to a family or a child, even though she will never be like mine. My children are so red-cheeked, so much like their father, so German, that they couldn't leave the homeland. They loved Brazil, where they were born, above all things. And I loved my freedom more than anything else.

The young woman returns, zipping up. The woman looks at her as if scolding her; the girl ignores it and throws herself onto the sofa. She has the same attitude I sense in Glorita when I ask her not to be late or to let me know if she has to run errands.

"Do you come every week?" I open my mouth again.

"Yes, and you?" She surprises me with a kinder tone.

"Me too."

"I had never seen you," she says.

"They changed our session from Thursday to Friday."

"Then we'll see each other next week," she concludes with a half-smile, grabbing her briefcase—she doesn't use a purse, but a briefcase—and pulling her granddaughter by the forearm. The granddaughter is a limp noodle who doesn't want to get up from the sofa.

"See you," I manage to say over Glorita's shoulder, who is already dragging her feet with glassy eyes, coming in high.

"You did it again!" I scold her.

"What do you care!?"

"I'm in charge of you until your parents come back."

"They're not coming back..."

"Of course they are! They're going to kick your ass."

The unoiled hinge of Dr. Retz's door makes that particular noise like a nail scratching a chalkboard, like Glorita trying to cut meat quickly, scraping the fork against the plate. The unoiled hinge of my life. The hasty departure on the plane, my children's snot, just snot, no words, no tears. A little German boy doesn't cry, and a little man doesn't cry—the words of my last husband. I remember the hands and embraces of the first one—the one I loved, the one who departed from me. Dr. Retz comes to get us; I hear him moving his obese body like someone pushing a wheelbarrow of cement. His heavy breathing, the ten steps between the waiting room and his office, the green mile where any day he might drop dead from the effort of welcoming his patients.

"How are you?" he asks without waiting for an answer. "Come in," he adds in his accented Spanish.

His blue eyes remind me of Hans. Hans Pérez is a half-Brazilian boy, half Jewish, and half German. When Pablo left me, I clung to Hans to make it seem like I was the one leaving him. Pablo has brown eyes and dark skin. The silly things I think about when Glorita explains to Dr. Retz her endless reasons for getting high again. As she goes over the list of complaints, which of course includes me, I feel Pablo's hands brushing my nipple, knowing that was the only way to turn me on; there was no other. Hans never figured it out, and I don't know how I ended up having three kids with him. "It's because of my parents, because of my parents," I hear Glorita excusing herself. "My parents, my ass," I think, and then Pablo's lips, the touch of his lips gently brushing against my nipple. Pablo.

"Could that be why?" Dr. Retz surprises me, pulling me out of those dark-skinned hips that knew so well how to move over me.

"What?"

"Could the relapse be because of the loss?"

My kids were beautiful; all three were rosy-cheeked and had brown eyes like mine. What beautiful children! What thick lips and slender limbs! What are they doing? What?

"We're going to try hypnotherapy, okay?" says Dr. Retz.

We all agree, but in the end, we know how the story goes. Glorita tries, stays clean for a couple of weeks, gets an itch, searches and finds my bottle of Vicodin for chronic pain, and relapses. She always finds the bottle, always! And could it be that my kids are sitting right now, on a similar couch, high? And somewhere, am I a grandmother with a rude granddaughter who pulls up her pants halfway between the bathroom and the waiting room? And somewhere, is there someone like me waiting, longing for an ex's bites?

"Do you want to start next week?" Dr. Retz is back.

"Yes, sure," I reply. As if it matters. Glorita will use again.

I get up from the chair very quickly, though I'm barely fifty. It's harder for Glorita; she struggles against gravity, grabs her butt, and the weekend looms ahead, with the shopping she'll want to do half high, half focused, the household chores I'll make her finish, and the long, hot shower I'll take with my hand between my legs, my thumb pretending to be Pablo in my crotch, while Glorita watches TV in the other room. She'll probably lose her job again; what will I tell my compadres? It would have been better if they had taken Glorita rather than left her here. If they had taken her, she wouldn't be like this, I think, trapped in a life with a godmother who doesn't even believe in God and who does nothing but yearn, because sometimes I feel an emptiness when I remember Pablo.

"How are you?" As soon as I see her sitting in the waiting room, I greet her immediately.

She's wearing the same black jacket with red trim. Her name is Lorenza; she tells me and shares the story of her life because she wants to talk or for some other reason.

She arrived 35 years ago, crossed the river on a raft, and was newly married at eighteen. Fear gripped them as they rowed, became trapped, swam, and fled into the woods to seek refuge. She no longer requires papers; she already has them. She had children and grandchildren; her family is *legal*. She built a miniature Mexica empire of backhoes, cranes, and construction materials. She is the owner and lady of her industry, employing a hundred people or more, a mother to seven children, and a grandmother to twenty-two grand-children. All of her children are healthy and responsible, with the exception of the youngest one. He shoots up whatever he finds, but why? The young girl with her pants halfway down is his daughter, rebellious because neither father nor mother have settled down. She has become the guardian. She tells me almost everything without breathing, afraid, it seems, of regretting it if she stops for a second to hear my opinion. I try to keep a serious face; I tend to smile at everything, and it's a great effort not to laugh or remember Pablo's white teeth biting my nipple. Her tone of voice softens and drops; I see her looking at the floor, as if searching for that imag-inary TV screen that the previous week had freed us from the obligation to talk.

"I'm very sorry," I say, somewhat nervously.

"Don't be sorry. No. People go astray for any reason; it's never anyone's fault."

I don't know how to respond; Lorenza has pride, some-thing I've traded for guilt. But suddenly, I feel that maybe there is a way out, that perhaps Glorita can recover, that it doesn't have to do with abandonment or loss or any of that, but with other things, because people go astray for any reason, for any reason. Maybe what I need to do is free myself from the lustful ghost of Pablo, who, it seems, wasn't that great, and those rosy-cheeked children who never loved me because I never really bore them, no matter how much I tell myself another story, and the few years we lived together they spent comparing me to their dead mother. I left, and in reality, there were no tears or snot; little men don't cry, nor do they want to cry.

People go astray for any reason.

I hear the hinge of Dr. Retz's door as he moves his barrel-like body, filled with lard and huffs.

"Are you ready?" he asks, standing in the doorway. I look around; there's no Glorita this morning, and I wonder if there will ever be Glorita again or if I'll let her rest along with the memory of my *compadres*, the three who were killed two years ago trying to cross the border.

"Yes," I reply and try to get up quickly, though I'm barely fifty and have the real desire to turn my life around.

"See you later." I stop to say goodbye to Lorenza.

She says, looking down at her phone, "See you later." Then she reacts, "Wait, what's your name?"

"Gloria," I answer, rubbing my back a bit because of the chronic pain, trying to quell the hunger for Vicodin.

*****

Comadre and *compadre* are godparents of a child.

4

Urban Safari

The problem is the expectations of meeting every standard: the upturned nose, the flat belly, the dyed blonde hair to look as much as possible like every golden American body around her because she's always demanded too much of herself since she was a child. Maybe then they'll start praising her—a round of applause here, a compliment there—no more pullovers or "license and registration." But it's not because she's brown-skinned, no sir; it's because as soon as she sees a police patrol, Pancha gets scared and tends to press the accelerator. Always vigilant, the only woman in the Montes de Oca family, who also turned out dark-skinned because of the crazed great-grandmother, the one who slept with the black men on the banana plantation—that's why she came out brown, and there's no L'Oreal Feria in the world that can lighten her hair. Pancha Montes de Oca, in her Land Rover, perpetually perched in her Jimmy Choo shoes, courtesy of

Pelado, her husband, talking on an unlimited plan phone, and her MK hanging from her shoulder. Hiding, if possible, the less glamorous past on the banana estate near Puerto Limón and dodging calls from relatives left open-mouthed, hungry birds waiting for the worm for her to send them all she earns, and she, in response, sends them nothing. She won't return to her village yet unless it's to buy the property titles that the hungry, arrogant relatives haven't sold yet, and she, in a final act of vindication, will sell to the highest bidder. She's good at business and at looking innocent, except when she's driving, but she'll find a way to leave them behind, along with that Caribbean past where, being the "black girl," she was sent to wash dishes, the Costa Rican Cinderella with wide hips and an upturned nose and a flat belly.

Already in Dallas, she has potential clients: her patients from the geriatric wing, the typical old folks who want to retire in the warm lands of Costa Rica, the happiest country in the world, "Yes, it is; look," she tells them, showing a photo of the farm where she grew up somewhat happy, though lonely. "And why did you come here?" To seek better horizons, Pancha replies, playing with the Cartier bracelet dangling from her wrist like a flag of conquest, the grand evidence that her decision was the right one and that the fight that erupted on the farm when she announced she was going to America wouldn't have etched two deep lines into her forehead.

Because the Montes de Oca had been the lords, masters of the Pacific, of Talamanca, and everyone who crossed their path for centuries, a saga of heroes resisting the decline of the banana industry for years, selling their lands to the new rich, to five-star hotels, investing in amusement parks, even returning protected forests to the Government, which so desired to build a nature sanctuary, for a price, of course. And when almost everything was gone, when there was almost no full udder left to suck from, the Montes de Oca retreated to the last farm, the one in Puerto Limón. There were great men, spreading wings and backs, and the black Pancha received what was good, amid slaps and one or two abuses smelling of rum and moonless nights; and what are you complaining about if the crazy great-grandmother slept with the blacks on the plantation? And maybe that's why, sometimes Pancha wonders, she likes old men more than young ones, because the worst and most insistent was her mother's sister's husband. And that's why she rejected Carlos's proposal, the young nurse at Texas Presbyterian Hospital, where she's been working for four years, to tie herself to Pelado, an old fat man skilled with his hands and whose generous checkbook Pancha has put on a diet, with safaris to the Galleria mall in downtown Dallas, hunting for bags and shoes. She will share the lands and profits with Pelado in exchange for citizenship. That will be soon. As soon as she gathers a little more money and courage, Pancha will play the role of the victim she so despises; the "I was raped" will run through the dining room in front of the not-so-surprised eyes of her older brothers, who, to silence the claim—and because the Montes de Oca don't do such filthy things—will give her whatever she wants, and what she wants, it's already said, is the lands.

It's just a matter of meeting expectations, staying cheerful, and rolling in dollars; she's demanded too much of herself since she was a child. Not pressing the accelerator when she sees a police officer, not starting the pull-over-and-license-and-registration dance again so she doesn't lose her green card, because, after all, she's a Montes de Oca, darker but also stronger and more determined. And very soon she will go to claim what's hers. Meanwhile, show me those shoes, no thank you, I'll try them on myself.

5

Water Bearer

Suddenly, she has been tasked with bringing the water. To summon it, to have it rise from the womb of the earth, from the bowels of her Loving Mother. Or to have it fall, transformed into droplets from the sky, and she runs to gather it between her fingers and transfer it from the stone to the leather bag. She must bring water for her village, for what remains of her village, and for the three families that survive like *llaretas*, growing green against the odds of the high plateau. Three families that resist the theft of the ancestral waters that once bathed the salt flats, life-giving water now used to wash minerals, degraded by the city men, water that cries deep beneath the earth, are now trying to hide.

Suddenly, she has been tasked with bringing the water, and it is a responsibility for which she feels unprepared. It was her father who did it, with the skill of the elders who know how to communicate in the liquid tongue and with the knowledge passed down from her grandfather, who in turn learned it from his father and from the third grandfather. And now it is her turn to invoke the Loving Mother. And she does not know how to do it.

Many suns pass, and the thirst grows. The greenery withers. The alpaca grows restless. The women watch her, wait for her, and urge her on, all in the silence of the mountain wind.

She understands that she cannot wait. She sets out at dawn to find the best cacti, the most even, the prickliest, the driest. She goes invoking the Loving Mother, stepping carefully, making herself stealthy so that the cactus does not escape. She climbs the first peak, but nothing. She climbs the second peak, but nothing. But on the third, there it is, nestled on the pinnacle of the sixth peak, the best cactus, even, prickly, and dry.

It will take hard work to reach it.

She adjusts her pack and launches herself at the conquest. And with each step she takes, she recalls her father's hands on that other cactus that used to bring water. Her father's hands removing each thorn, just as her grandfather did, as did his father and the third grandfather. Smoothing the roughness until it was soft and smooth like the skin of her cheeks. "See?" he said, making her feel that softness, one of the few times she did not miss the desert's roughness. And just like that, still unsure, on the pinnacle of the sixth peak, she carefully and laboriously cuts the cactus with a small but sharp knife, and she begins to strip it of every needle and of its natural defenses. She saves the thorns to dry them in the sun and then puts them inside, in the cactus that will become a cylinder, a container, a resonant song, of rain, of the promise of rain, or a stream. Thorns and seeds that she will later include—the same secret seeds that her father once preserved inside—before her amazed childhood eyes when it was his turn to bring the water.

The sun is setting, and she must return to the village. She puts the knife in her pack, and she puts the thorns in her pack. She grabs the hollow cactus, the container, and raises it at sunset to offer it to Inti, the great God, so that the great God will preserve it with his golden fingers.

She descends from the sixth peak. She counts the steps that separate her from the village. Many still. She must hurry if she does not want to face the highland's cold. She will follow the golden fingers of the great God, who is always a good guide and will lead her back.

Suddenly, she was tasked with bringing the water when, in disputes with the miners, her father was killed. And she does not know how to do it, but she feels, and she learns, that the newly conquered cactus will become a Water Stick. And that the cactus will converse with the hidden springs deep and high using liquid tongues, much like a Water Stick. And thus, it will rise from the bowels of the Loving Mother or fall in the form of droplets from the sky. And in the moment the miracle happens, new pages will be written in the books of her lineage, newly inaugurated stories that will tell that she was the first girl who managed to speak with the waters.

*****

Llareta: a slow-growing, cushion-like plant found in the high-altitude regions of the Andes, known for its dense, green, and moss-like appearance.

6

"   "

It's been three days that my hair has the shape of head-phones. This happens to me because I don't invest in haircuts; I enter the first place that has a barber available. I know this because someone grabs my arm and leads me to a free chair in no time. That's why my hair is flat on the crown of my head and puffs out at ear level. In short, because I didn't tell the man what I needed.

I still have misunderstandings because God gave me a mouth but not speech.

Because I hear, but I don't listen.

I have big eyes, but I'm extremely nearsighted.

That's why I constantly fall. I laugh, but there is sadness in the laughter. And my soul hurts. I try not to be melodramatic, but I bump into people on the streets, and they shout angrily, "Watch where you're going!"

The cane helps geographically, but not in virtue. "Can I help you, grandma?" they ask me. I've only carried thirty years on my back, but this long, rubber-handled, metal cane for the blind puts me in another category.

I don't complain about my nose because it's the only thing that works.

I wasn't always like this. There was a time when I could see, hear, and speak. But that happened many seasons ago, before my nose took command of everything. Now, with my sense of smell, I navigate the city; I have a map of scents that leads me from the bakery to the pharmacy to the greengrocer. The stench signals what I'm looking for, the people I need, and the purchases I need to make.

Two blocks from my house, there's a drain and a traffic light that I can't distinguish. Apparently, there's a bridge because at that corner the asphalt vibrates, and the fierce traffic churns my stomach. I don't set foot on the pavement because the sewer's stench warns me of danger. I wait a bit until someone offers to help me cross. The person purrs next to me. They don't know that I can't decipher their sounds. I smile. I've gotten used to smiling. Or, to what I remember, a grimace that split the face in two, a gesture people used to interpret as something good. I rely on that memory to respond to others.

On the next sidewalk, I perceive a slight acidity, so I move forward. The helper leaves me there; I feel the pressure of their hand on my elbow. That smell of damp pine recedes; it was a young man. I try to hold on to that clearing in the forest of stinks, but the tiny blades of ammonia cut through the wood.

I'm already at the corner of urine. There's a unique spot in Laurides where the waste of dogs, drunks, and children combines—a vertex where we are all the same yellowish filth.

Now that I've reached my destination, I know Beatriz will appear in a few minutes. She always comes on time. She understands my problem. She knows this caustic point in the neighborhood isn't the best waiting room.

The fresh lavender swaying in the meadow precedes her, and when she greets me, a kiss on the cheek, I know she's wearing her "French Rose" lipstick. Beatriz is beautiful, I know because no ugly person smells good.

"What happened to you?" she asks, touching the ends of my hair.

"Nothing..." I say, ignoring the allusion to my bad haircut.

Beatriz doesn't insist.

That's what I like about her—her discretion. That and the smell of a French meadow. I've sensed it before in the pharmacy two stinks away from my house. The clerk, a woman who must be pretty, applies the same cologne, so I recognize her. She makes sure to attract me like a mosquito to sweet mango, either out of pity or because I'm a good customer. Several times I've thought of buying a bottle of perfume for Beatriz; it would be a good gift. Every time she opened the bottle, the fragrance would be released in high, round, whitish curls. I think it would make her happy.

Beatriz helps me up the stairs; the worn rubber of the steps smells like a newly bought doll. We enter her office, where the azaleas dance to a purple rhythm, as usual. Beatriz is mountain flowers, the warm embrace of her arm linked with mine, the apathetic familiarity of someone who doesn't know me but at the same time knows so much about me.

"What are we doing today?" I ask her.

"More tests, Manuela. We still can't understand why you can't see, even if, clinically, you have perfect vision. Your myopia has no explanation. And your hearing is perfect, but..."

Beatriz's voice fades inside me. It's not the first time I've heard these words. Rows of doctors, vanilla, coffee, tobacco, and mint candies have told me the same. Beatriz is my last hope. The best, said the doctor, who loved pickled onions, and every time he spoke to me, I felt nauseous. "Visit her," he insisted, "and I'm sorry I couldn't help you," he concluded in an acrid breath.

"Manuela?" I hear her repeat.

Her silhouette becomes even blurrier.

I only manage to smell her once more before entering my silence.

I coil up and go inward.

Because I choose. I choose not to listen, not to see, and not to speak. Because I carry a world tangled in my hair—a space of pain impossible to share. That must remain hidden at all costs, even at the expense of bad haircuts and weekly visits to Dr. Beatriz.

This is easier than accepting the truth that breathes beneath the navel. That pricks and reminds. That closes the ears, the eyes, and the mouth. That takes away speech. Better than revisiting the trampled back of my being, simpler than polishing the calluses that have emerged in my will. Blocking the bitter attacks on my youthful body, bloodied thighs. The horror.

This is better.

I don't hear, I don't see, I don't speak.

I don't tell you.

7

Dorotea Chained

There has been silence since they gave her the pills. A silence hangs from the fan. She has been bedridden for months, on a bed of nails that pierce her buttocks, back, and heels. Silence and pills are medicine to calm the soul. She doesn't understand why she talks to herself; it wasn't like this before. Before, she was agile and beautiful on the cold coasts of Quintero, legs, arms, and long hair. Before, she was concrete and didn't say silly things like "quiet the soul." She loses herself in the silence of the blades of that thing screwed to the ceiling, the branches of a mechanical tree reaching to grab her. From hair once golden, now ashen, the fan-tree grabs her to take her away, maybe back to Quintero. She doesn't know how she got here, either. Wasn't it yesterday that I left my husband behind? Didn't Benjamín cry at the sound of the plane? Didn't I bring a shopping list? Where is the shopping list? With the claw of the fan seeking her and the air turbine wanting to suck her in, Benjamín latched to her nipple, not sucking, just playing. No more, Benjita; no more, baby. The pills and the silence.

Robbery at the gas station. Have I been there? The news on television yells that a masked man shot the clerk, and they arrested him. She thinks they once stopped at that same corner. Benjita wanted to buy a drink. Was I robbed? She asks the white-clad figure, insisting on giving her pills. A clockwork figure appears at four chimes. How did I get out? Did you find me? The figure with her hands grabs her nose to cut off her breath and force her to swallow the pink pills—no water, no time for water. Only the cold waters of the Quintero coast. Silence again when what she wants is to hear.

> A house of red bricks, brown tiles, a yellow wall. A lawn that insists on dying during the summer. The thorny, twisted tree that is never thirsty. The ugly flowers that grow from artichoke-like plants, a feast for bees. She agile, on her knees, battling against the weeds. She, in a place of thorny trees, is tough like the weeds. She misses the pines, the eucalyptus, the expansive breathing invaded by droplets, the Pacific encapsulated in the marine vapor.

A fire, an apartment burning. Have I been there? The news on television yells that someone forgot to unplug a coffee maker and that miraculously, the fire was contained. Benjita's birthday, thirty candles, the cake in flames. The brown figure, smelling of food, appears at the foot of her bed. I'm not injured; did I live there? Did you like the chocolate cake? The brown figure maneuvers, and the humming bed rises. Her back adjusts, glued to the sheet, sweating, and no one changes her. Water, she says, water on the back. No time for water, only mush, because apparently there are no teeth either. Did I lose my teeth? The brown figure withdraws, leaving behind its stew-like stench.

A lucid dream at last. The brown figure forgot to lay her down. The blind is open, many clouds, cottony, it seems to be raining, it seems to be thundering. Finally, there is noise. Voices, figures, and more figures circulate in the hallway outside her room. She moves her legs, she feels them. She rejoices with the vitality she had when she left Benjita and her husband in Quintero. She moves her arms; she feels them. She breathes in with the strength she had when swimming, regardless of the cold Pacific water. She feels her buttocks, they have no thorns. But the sweat bathing her back persists. She turns to lower her legs. She places her feet on the ground, not remembering the last time she walked. Before the first silence pill, yes, before... She dares to stand up, holding onto the bed rail, and sees her reflection in the window—a face of wrinkles and many laughs—that's what she sees. Beyond that, the swirling, greenish sky announces a tornado.

A house of red bricks, brown tiles, a wall that was yellow but should have been painted green. Arched trees that don't die. Bees making hives in the gutter. They are not bees, they are wasps! Burning, ice water, help!, there is no one. Benjamín got married and left. The house returns the echo of her former voice, which was confident and determined. The swollen finger, the wasp's feast starts to close her throat. She will have to go to the hospital alone.

Is it because of the wasp sting? Is that why I'm here? She anxiously asks the white figure reappearing with its fine, rigid hands, always on time, to lay her down again, to lower the bed's backrest, and to tuck her in as tightly as if wishing to immobilize her.

Seek shelter now. Tornado. Now. Is it because of the wasp? The news on television yells that a tornado is approaching; it has lifted roofs, overturned cars, flooded schools. She remembers her granddaughters, Benjita's daughters, being scared the first weekend they stayed with her—a Saturday of alarms and howling winds—the four of them hiding in the bathtub. Was it the tornado that brought me here? She wonders, clinging to the time when she didn't talk to herself and didn't say "quiet the soul," the time when Benjamín also left Quintero to join her in Texas. The happy time when she thought she still had a husband back in Chile, only to discover later that it didn't exist and that what was called love had dried up with the pine tree that provided good shade in a house now sheltering someone else. When the windowpane shakes, the hail is a swarm of ice-bird fury, and the green tornado sky looms overhead, she remembers that it was Benjamín, her Benjita, who put her in the hospice. Before she lost her words, before memories tangled, before she believed she was Dorotea searching for the wizard, before all that, she was a woman. She screams, but the ceiling fan catches her. She screams, and her hair burns at the roots. Then the pills, the white figure pinching her nose, forcing her to swallow the pills of silence, tying her hands, and speaking softly, as if the white figure cared, just a bit, about what hurt her. And what hurts her, in the moment of the scream, is oblivion.

8

Ramona in Duet

I Ramona from Here

Ramona packs, watching the clock, counting every minute of that annoying tick, that metallic contraption with tangled guts, the thing her grandmother keeps in the dining room/ living room/lounge, all that fits in those four by four meters, four walls, four o'clock. Ramona packs, watching the clock.

The grandmother enters, at the same time as always, stereotypical grandmother, little old lady with gray hair but a blackened heart. There is no other choice, she said. You're leaving, and you're leaving soon; that's it. No more romance novels, you're leaving. So Ramona packs at four o'clock in those four walls. She already knows she's been sold and maybe it was for four coins. And she's hungry and understands that this hunger, the cramp, the hunger, will grow slowly and quietly until it bursts forth on the other side of the river, the Grande. The hunger, the cramp.

It's time, It's time. A while ago, says the grandmother, who looks at her with disgust, with a silent fury that hangs like tiny hands from the vein in her neck, and from those temples that were once smooth, like a vast desert where there was no room for hatred, the resentment of being left with this granddaughter, Ramona, this Ramona anchored to the lap of a grandmother with a blackened heart. That's it—a package, this Ramona. A bargaining chip. Wide hips, Ramona, neither dumb nor a genius, Ramona. Good haunches, don't you see? Four coins: gold, silver, tin. It doesn't matter, just take her away. Yes, surely over there, they'll find her mother, because the father is already dead, already shot, already lying in the ditch, in the dump, in the desert behind the house, between the town and the border, in El Paso. Around there, he must be. This is the grandmother, the wolf, and the red riding hood, and instead of baskets, coins.

Ramona packs, tick-tock, tick-tock, rustle rustle, rolling up what little she has, keeping that crucifix, to save her, to protect her. Tick-tock, rustle, rustle. Ramona packs under the burning eyes of the grandmother, saying that it's time, that it's the same time, and that they're coming, Ramona. And Ramona just blinks, more and more slowly; it seems she can no longer see. She goes inward, to a very long and very blue sea, a sea where the Niña and the Pinta and the Santa María cross, a lost ship, the arrival in America, paradise, and four o'clock.

II Ramona from There

Black, curly hair. Thick, red lips. Round, warm, plump hips. Ramona. Agile mind, precise words, once silent in front of the grandmother, now eloquent. Ramona. She towers over sixteen on the other side. Ramona pays attention, she was sent to die, she has no desire to. She pays attention and repeats, a parrot, Ramona. From her thick, red lips emerges a newly inaugurated kingdom, paradise, the crossing, the Niña, the Pinta, the Santa María; they leave her on the other side. Nobody cares if she makes it, but she doesn't die, Ramona; she has no desire to.

Stubborn Ramona.

Ramona learns, creates, Ramona gathers new sounds. Round hips, they want to marry her off. But she has no desire to. She wants to keep stringing syllables together like beads on a new necklace, which gradually forms day by day. A necklace where everything sounds different, even the most trivial things. Marriage is the most trivial thing. Sex, the most trivial thing. Hands on her hard breasts, the most trivial thing. Ramona doesn't want to sell herself; she has no desire.

Ramona wants to adorn herself with this new necklace and hang more words, nouns, and verbs until she reaches sentences, creating a twenty-turn necklace with twenty sentences. Forty turns, forty sentences. A necklace so long, endless, woven with the language that resides on the other side.

Longer than the sea she crossed, more powerful than the waves that wouldn't let her reach the shore. Ramona learns, agile mind, precise words. Ramona wasn't dumb, but a jeweler, and she'll keep threading beads and words, she'll keep tying knots and clasps to the jewel of her new language. She'll craft a bracelet of nouns, a tiara of adjectives, and a belt of pronouns, she'll sew garments of affirmations and a purple cape of readings, she'll weave her own path, where there is no room for the grandmother. A path just for her, without gold, silver, or tin coins, without packing in four walls at four o'clock, rustle rustle, without rosaries, rustle rustle, without baskets, tick-tock. Without grandmothers with blackened hearts. And she'll do all this with her tongue, with her new tongue, with her double tongue, and she'll do all this because she wants to.

9

Harvest

My father settled in San Mittre de Laurides because of the cemetery, which is near a grove, and its shade keeps it between five and seven degrees cooler than the rest of the town. That's why my father came, because the chill was such that the deceased almost daily emerged from their graves in search of warmth. He says that when he arrived in San Mittre, following the newspaper advertisement, the mayor was so happy to see him that he gave him a welcoming hug and hired him in less than ten minutes.

My father says the town square reverberated with such a peculiar noise, as if jugs full of water were breaking; it was so annoying that it soon gave him a headache. "The noise is not the biggest problem," the mayor told him, "compared to the Harvest." Before he arrived, the town had tried various mechanisms to select the person in charge; they held raffles and jumping competitions, selected by finger-pointing, but no one wanted to do it. Orietta, the oldest neighbor, had suggested placing an ad in the local weekly. For two reasons, she said: she was tired of the late Fuentes leaving his jawbone in her front yard. And that she would join the parade of the dead and better have it organized who would pick her up at the end of each day.

My father had left my grandfather's farm a few months earlier, but after a short journey, his dreams of fame and fortune had dwindled to sleeping under the Laurimague creek bridge, wrapped in newspapers.

One night of extreme cold, with a tiny bonfire barely warming his hands, he stumbled upon the ad Orietta had placed.

"Collector needed. Good pay. House and Food," he read. "Collecting fruits," my father thought before falling asleep; he was good at that, much to his chagrin. When he woke up, he headed to town, thinking he would find a regiment of fruit pickers and would have to show off his strength to get the job. However, to his surprise, he was the only applicant, and the mayor, as I said, received him with open arms.

That same afternoon, as the sun set, with the town enveloped in a wintery glaze and all its inhabitants already in their homes, huddled around stoves, the mayor asked him to wait in the center of the square, saying they would come soon, and then he left. "The bosses," my father thought.

The dull sound against the cobblestones of the town, which he had heard all afternoon, gradually increased until it became deafening. It was a procession of skeletons emerging from the four corners of the square and heading to the cemetery. "The Harvest..." my father understood, and with the practical sense that characterized him, he followed the parade, picking up jaws, femurs, phalanges, and all bone fragments that were falling. He followed them to the cemetery, confirmed it was freezing, saw each one enter a grave, and then he went in, returning bones somewhat at random.

After finishing, he made his way to the new house that the mayor had earlier shown him. The little house next to the cemetery was comfortable, warm, and dry. The smell of onions and carrots simmering in the pot comforted him. He ate, went to bed, and fell asleep immediately. I already mentioned that my father is not one to complicate his life. Staying there instead of giving up and going back to my grandfather's farm was obviously the best course of action.

At the crowing of the rooster, Orietta's singing voice woke him through the window. She wanted to thank him because her flowers had bloomed vibrant, open, and free of teeth. Soon, all of his neighbors—barely a hundred people—were surrounding him. The whole town was satisfied and started planning a big feast. Enthusiastic about his new skills, my father quickly became an expert in the "Harvest" and boasted of not forgetting any bones. Thus, his life began to flow with the sweet routine of work.

My father says he met my mother during one of those rounds. At first, she followed him a couple of blocks, then some kilometers, and finally all the way to the cemetery while he pushed the cart to finish the job before nightfall. It amused him to have this company. When he could, he turned to look at her, and what he liked most about her were her rosy cheeks and crimson lips. Thus, between smiles and a few words, one night they made love surrounded by half-open graves.

Very soon, I was born, and happiness was complete. But one fine day, when my first two teeth were coming in, my father found me sucking on a clavicle, trying to ease the gum itching. Then he thought it was time to change fields; after all, he had a family now, had a daughter, and wanted to have more.

In the following months, he set himself to the task of saving to get us out of the town as soon as possible, and when he had saved enough money, he informed the mayor that we would be leaving. The man begged us to stay; I remember because everyone showed up at the house, but this time they were less festive. Orietta whimpered at the news. A man with a wooden leg raised his fists, and I ran to hide behind my father. After much commotion, the mayor said my father was, without a doubt, the best collector the town had ever seen. "Without comparison," the townspeople added in unison, in a strange chorus of voices indicating they did not accept the resignation.

My father suggested closing the cemetery. The mayor refused. My father proposed cutting down the trees, installing boilers, and raising a fence high enough to block the mountain wind, but none of the ideas caught on. They wanted my father, and my father insisted that we had to leave. The mayor gave in, thankfully, and turned around; the townspeople followed, introspective, with stiff shoulders, occasionally complaining and insulting us.

My mother, who had observed everything from the window, was a little uneasy when we entered the house. "Are you sure?" she asked. My father only responded with a nod. The plan was to leave after breakfast. My mother moved silently, though her hands trembled a bit, and with her typical frugality, she packed only the essentials in a trunk.

At dusk, suddenly, my mother was gone. I was small; I don't remember many details, but my father returned from his last harvest and found me alone at home. He waited for a while, but my mother did not come, so we silently ate the stew she had left cooking on the stove. Later, I discovered that my father stayed up all night waiting for her until he heard murmurs in the early hours, then a loud bang against the door. He ran to open it, and there she was, sitting on the ground, pale, her cheeks gray, and her lips blue, her gaze fixed, frozen, somewhat horrified.

At dawn, her death became known, and the town showered us with attention. Orietta even appeared with a handmade scarf, which she lovingly wrapped around my mother's neck, covering those purple marks like a rope that had appeared there. True, my father was devastated, and when the town offered to bury mom for free and even significantly increased his salary, in the confusion of loss, he accepted.

At times, at meal time, he becomes regretful and tells me he should have taken us away secretly so that we would still be together. He cries and laments not having done so.

Then I remind him that we still are, the three of us, and that we just have to wait until the next morning, when my mother comes out to seek the sun, and he, at the end of the day, collects her and returns her to her grave.

Highlighted Stories

Selection of award winning short stories

10

María Kawésqar

I am the first woman after a long line of men. I am the fulfillment of my grandmother, the utmost, absolute, and most beloved fulfillment of my grandmother. My name is Maria Kawésqar, and I am going to tell you my story. I don't expect you to believe me; you know, when you have so many years behind you, you invent. It is most likely that I invented the name Maria too, because I never knew my original name. I was born in the south in a cold country with rains, mountains, channels, and cold forests. In my head, I carry the stories of my grandparents, my mothers, uncles, sisters, and children, and that is the story I want to tell you. It is brief; don't despair; it will only take a blink of an eye.

We were thousands, the people of my kingdom, strong masters and owners of the lands where the world ends. We spoke to the mountains, and they rose to stop the rains coming from the other side; thus, we obtained milder winters. The ocean calmed its waves at our command to let us see the jumping, silvery fish, ready to be gathered. The children ran barefoot and naked, collecting sea fruits, in a joy and embrace so natural that we never imagined life could be lived any other way.

That was my people until the invader arrived, first with bronze helmets, mustaches, and armored chests. Later in ships, metal whales captured aquatic life without following rhythm or moon. We fought and struggled; we resisted for years against these skinny, pale beings who attacked us with gunpowder, rabid dogs, nets, and harpoons. Little by little, our energy waned, and our young people died. Instead of exterminating us, the invader committed the most horrendous act: they forcefully took us and threw us into the belly of their metal whale, to sail for centuries to distant lands, to kingdoms with strange tongues, where they wore heavy clothes and sea wolf skins were not enough. Lands of souls so empty that they required so much, so much to survive. There, I heard the roar of the train and lamented the height of the brick and stone buildings that the wretched souls had built. What pity I felt for them! How much the pale man needs to be happy! Very soon, they took us to exhibitions and displayed us like trade animals. Lifeless faces stared at us from the other side of the cage, and we were held by the wrists with heavy chains. They did not understand us; they do not know what they have lost...

I don't know how much time passed before we could

return. A handful survived the return journey, and those who came back sick infected the few who had stayed. Then I took over the leadership. I gathered the girls and the old women, and we went to the hidden caves, those known only to us. Things seemed to be going well in that newly founded kingdom, but the pale man's disease reached us there too, and they began to die. It must have been the lack of common blood among our fathers, husbands, and children; the lack became a wound, and my women bled out, withering in the sight and indifference of a timid winter sun. Thus, I became what I am now, without smell, without sight, but the last and the keeper of our stories. Maria Kawésqar. The only thing left of that vast kingdom was the memory of the icy valleys that we commanded with our voices.

Since my own disappeared, I have gone from village to village, sharing what I have seen and heard—the fights I have fought, the scars on my calves from lashes and battles. I survived, and I think we all survived, as long as I continue wandering the world, sitting down to talk with you, and as long as you listen to the stories of my people—of those brave and fierce ones who died, of those who were taken as curiosities to dead lands and managed to return. More than five hundred years have passed, but we are still alive. Before my memory, the invader weakens and becomes a cockroach that I crush with a finger. Our resistance is harder, stronger, and more determined. And so is my memory.

* * * * *

"María Kawésqar" (original Spanish version) won first place People's Choice and Honorable Mention by the jury in Hispanic Heritage Literature Organization, Miami, USA.

The Kawésqar are an indigenous people who inhabit the south of Chile. This story is a free interpretation of the events they have had to face.

11

The summer of Alfonsina

Alfonsina bathed in this sea when she came incognito to the beaches of Quellón, and it was a great event for me to see her arrive with her little purple velvet suitcase, black woolen shawl, and round glasses that covered almost her entire face. "Alfonsina!" I wanted to shout when I saw her pass by, but I didn't dare interrupt her on her way between the guesthouse she rented at the back of Gutiérrez's property and the landing area. My shop was between her two destinations, and when she approached, I ran to hide behind the counter. What an idiot! From my hiding place, I looked at her boots. They were good and well-sewn; there was no hope that Alfonsina would stop in my shop. What I would have said if she ever showed up barefoot, her worn-out shoes hanging from her pale hand, I'll never know.

Alfonsina surely thought that no one knew her in Quellón,

but I did, the cobbler who also worked as a telegraphist, and it was pure luck that I found out about her visit. It rained when she got off the boat, and it was the height of summer. My colleague in Puerto Montt gave me the tip, who, in turn, received the news from the colleague in Concepción, and thus a long line of gossipers until it reached the telegraphist who saw her leave Montevideo with the same velvet suitcase with which she crossed the main street and asked the first person who smiled at her about Gutiérrez's property. I suppose she was looking for solitude, of course, because, in the end, where could she be more alone than on this island? I remember when Puerto Montt told me about Alfonsina; I thought she was a radio theater artist. It was because the colleague was very enthusiastic and didn't limit himself to dots and dashes but used full words to describe her. He had seen her get off the train at the station and stealthily followed her to the port, to see her depart wrapped in her shawl, standing on the bow, ready to cross the strait. When I saw her, it was indeed a spectacle, but not to my taste because the woman didn't have much meat on her bones. But enthusiasm is contagious, so I was just as excited to see her arrive. Very soon, I asked Puerto Montt who the hell the skinny woman was. Then he told me she was a poet and even transmitted a poem to me. It must be that I always had a romantic side, because the truth is that when I read those words that Puerto Montt sent me, which became a melody in my ears, oh boy, how my heart jumped, and I started crying like a little kid.

I never knew how Puerto Montt found out about her if, not long ago, he was transmitting the Twenty Poems to me, because according to him, Gloria, the baker's daughter, would easily give herself to me if I read them to her. However, Gloria that summer was one of those women who would not undress, not even for the great Neruda himself, so I decided not to waste time on her and instead fell in love with Alfonsina, spying on her during her fleeting strolls down the main street in silence. Buying bread every morning under Gloria's suspicious gaze and having dinner with the Gutiérrez family every evening... The Gutiérrez, a bunch of prudes, there was no way to get them to talk about what she was like behind closed doors. And she swam on the beach at dawn every one of the twenty-three days she stayed.

I dedicated myself to sending daily reports to Puerto Montt, who in turn retransmitted them to infinity. Thus, Alfonsina traveled in a chain of dots and dashes that anchored her life in some way because she seemed very volatile. Indeed, it was as if the kilo of bread she carried down the main avenue was the only weight that held her to the earth.

I won't say I prepared to talk to her; I wouldn't have known what to say. If I had opened my mouth, the grunts of the good donkey I've always been would have come out. So, I started writing to her: letters, poems, and reflections. If that Neruda guy could do it, why couldn't I? Although I never gave her any of my papers, no matter how hard I tried, very soon I saw her leave, and with that, the town shrank so much that my island felt like a prison. Of course, I regretted it and still regret it because even the dumbest person can say "Good morning." Puerto Montt laughed when I told him I froze in her presence, but then he said he understood, because he didn't say a peep either when she disembarked on the other side and boarded the train.

The following months without Alfonsina were the worst plague to hit Quellón. Gloria had no charm and was so heavy, plump, gossipy, and ill-tempered that I felt like closing the shop and leaving. The Gutiérrez never broke their silence, no matter how many free shoes and telegrams I offered. My only comfort was Puerto Montt's transmissions—the verses that had come from her hand. When the weather got better, I went to the landing every day, but nothing—not even the Pincoya appeared. I started eating less and worrying more because I had never felt so lovesick, not even when Gloria finally let me grab half a buttock, and, boy, it was hard to let go. It was around that time that Puerto Montt sent me the fateful notice that she had taken her own life, Alfonsina, that she had chosen to go with the sea, but not with my sea, and that hurt like a mule's kick because my sea is bold, cold, blue, and with no return. That dark afternoon, sitting next to the telegraph that was strangely silent as if it were also in mourning, I uncorked a bottle and started drinking until Gloria, all prim and proper, came and agreed to give me her whole buttock.

Weeks later, Puerto Montt tried to send me one of Alfonsina's books, but since the shipping was very expensive, he kept it for himself. Just excuses! I did keep, however, every one of the telegrams my colleague sent me.

I don't even remember how many years have passed—certainly more than twenty. But even now, when summer comes and the morning shines like today, I get a little gloomy, then I open the wooden box and rummage through Alfonsina's signs. Still, just in case, I keep an eye out for the boat. Who knows if it was all a mistake and one morning she'll get off wrapped in her shawl, dragging her bony body and suitcase, with that sad air she had, walking as if life wasn't worth anything.

*****

"El verano de Alfonsina" (original Spanish version) won second place in the II Litteratura Short Story Contest, held biennially by Litteratura. Barcelona, Spain.

Note from the author: Alfonsina Storni was an influential Argentine poet and playwright known for her modernist works and feminist themes; she tragically died by suicide, walking into the sea at Mar del Plata in 1938.

12

Neighborhood Typography

Josué smells like eucalyptus because he is allergic to India ink and spends his workday chewing medicinal candies. Josué moves slowly among the sheets hanging from clotheslines, navigating the workshop like freshly washed clothes, ready to be printed.

He thinks of his mother and her insistence on hand-washing his white shirt with puffed sleeves, the one he always wears on Thursdays. He takes extra care to move between the rows of rollers, types, and plates, which drip black blood.

At that hour, the backroom is a symphony of metallic sounds, with Josué, in the dim light, feeling around the boxes for the necessary molds. Like a blind man reading fortunes in runes, Josué recognizes each letter. He knows that the "A" is sharp and that the "Y" has an edge that cuts, weighing 20 grams.

Shortly after dawn, the sticky oil cylinder starts inking the plates. Josué feels hot, and at that hour, the once-elusive sun streams fully through the windows. The heat burns his ears, turning them red and sweaty.

In the small hell of his workshop, a smile spreads across his face; he knows his favorite part is coming. His shoulders move in sync with the plate, transferring paragraphs to the sheet. "The word is made," he murmurs while checking the first copies.

Outside, the laughter of children heading to school reminds him that he must hurry if he wants to offer the new bulletin at the corner grocery store.

He still needs to wait for the pamphlets to dry. He takes his morning coffee mug; the porcelain is cold, but he drinks it anyway, tasting bitter, like India ink. He figures that in ten minutes, his newspaper will be ready. He will move among the sheets, unhooking the pages, lay them out one over the other like someone preparing to roll cigarettes, and collate them, suddenly hearing Mercedes' heels clicking on the pavement, minutes before eight thirty. Then he will compile the most recent baby photos, the grocer's opinion, Jaimito's drawing, and the bunches of local news that include the fresh fruits of the community's imagination, such as the poems that crazy Lalo sent. Finally, without needing to turn off the light because it was never on, he will take his cane, which is always hanging by the door, and go outside to deliver his news, stumbling a little at first but soon walking like an expert thanks to the memory of his feet.

*****

"Tipografía de barrio" (original Spanish version) was a finalist and published with the winners of the I Short Story Contest by Zenú Publishing House: Homage to Gabriel García Márquez, Bogotá, Colombia.

Told from
the Hips

Selection of short stories from "Cuentos encaderados"
(Told from the hips)

13

The blood and the scape

For Thérèse

Vicente told me not to put my shoes on until I got to the station. If I arrive with dirty shoes, they'll suspect something. I'll be fine in first class. And that I should throw the nun's habit away. Otherwise, they'll be suspicious. I'm tired, and it's so dark I can barely see anything. Only the shadows of the trees under the moon. My feet are already starting to hurt. Walking without shoes, like the nuns, but over rocks, branches, and mud. There is so much farther to go. Vicente told me I would get there in about an hour. For sure. And on the other side, I'll be fine, yes, because over there, life is different and women can do whatever they want. They live their lives, and nobody controls them. And no one declares them insane. And they don't give up anything! Not even their daughters. Or their freedom. I couldn't, however, forgive myself if my daughter turned out to be a bastard. She cried so much. I withstood the tears. "Mommy's not crazy; she's just going away for a while," I repeated to her when they came to get me, while the "lump" that is my husband held her firmly so she wouldn't run towards me. It was best this way. If I didn't leave, the "lump" would condemn me and declare her a bastard. And she cannot grow up without a last name. No. Not here she can't; that's why I let her go and turned myself in, because this country is so minuscule she must keep her last name to grow up in safety, marry well and want for nothing. My feet are still painfully bleeding, of course, without shoes. I heard the "lump" tell her I was quite ill and that I must go to the hospital...

The stream... There must be about forty minutes to go.

Keep walking. I begged the "lump" to bring her to the convent to visit me, but he wouldn't. He didn't let me write to her either. They put me in a cell of windowless walls with just enough space for the bed and the winter fireplace. A jail-like door, no privacy. But it didn't matter because I could write to my daughter in secret with the paper, ink, and quill that my friend, one of the novices, had brought me after much begging. From the other side, I'll send her all these letters. My daughter will be delighted. She'll see her mother isn't ill, as she was told, and will soon come back for her. For now, I must keep walking. I must forget the pain in my ankle. And the "lump's" evil look as he bellowed out that the girl had forgotten me. The blood. My heels are bleeding.

The water mill... There must only be about twenty minutes to go.

Keep walking. On the "lump's" last visit, he found me cheerful. It was because of the letters I was writing my daughter, but I refused to tell him.

"What are you doing?!" he screamed, outraged. "Nothing," I answered. "Can't you see there's nothing here? No books, nothing."

But he thought it was because of Vicente, and he went mad again, just like he did when he found my notebooks hidden in the toy chest, and, in spite of fighting him to get them back, I couldn't manage it. He locked himself in his study, and I heard how he ripped out the pages and, I think, threw them into the fireplace. He came out of the study without looking at me and locked the door again. He had just found out about my writing and Vicente, and he immediately made plans for my banishment. The next morning, they took me to the convent. Keep walking. After the "lump's" visit, I was forbidden to talk to anybody. My novice friend was expelled, and the nuns would not speak to me, either. Only the other lunatics, the ones that are really crazy, came to me: they would brush my hair, sing to me, and try to coax me into playing with them. Then Vicente reappeared, when I no longer expected him, when I had already dried up after so much crying. After months of not having any news from him, there he was. Pay no attention to the blood, although, of course, it must hurt...

The crossroad... It should be close. Ten minutes. Keep walking.

My Vicente. I didn't recognize him dressed as a priest. "We don't have much time," he told me. He seemed serious. "Put it on," he said as he gave me a package. It had a dress and a nun's habit inside. I put on the dress and then the habit, one on top of the other, in front of Vicente. He didn't look away. He stared at me the whole time. Then he asked me to follow him, head bowed down. So I did. We proceeded through the central corridor, with its windows overlooking the courtyard. The nuns were right there, working in the vegetable patch. We continued to the chapel, which was empty at that time of day, and from there into the street. I couldn't believe it. I was free at last! Outside was a cart filled with hay. We got on, and Vicente set off quickly. There were so many things I wanted to say to him, but I couldn't. I remained silent. I tried to thank him, but instead I just watched him. He was focused on guiding the horse until we eventually stopped at the entrance to this road, which I already knew because this was where we used to meet. We got down from the cart, and he told me to go straight for an hour without straying from the path, that once I was past the crossroad, the station would be very close, and that the train to Buenos Aires would be about to depart. He gave me a pair of shoes and a first-class ticket. He told me not to talk to anyone and not to look at anybody. "Even if they look at you, Teresita," he said, smiling and a bit sad. I asked him to come with me. "I can't," he answered. I asked him to take care of my daughter. "I can't," he repeated. Then I turned my back to him, this time forever. I started to walk. And I cried. Probably for my daughter. The grief sank down to my heels, and they bled. Keep walking. I must be close. Now...

Yes! The station!

VICENTE

I didn't have time to explain anything. She wouldn't have understood anyway. They had already declared her insane. There was nothing left to do. Getting near the convent was difficult. I was being watched. At the entrance to my house, there was always a carriage with two men, day and night, immovable. It took me months to plan the escape. The hardest part was getting the nun's habit. But she wouldn't understand. She wouldn't know what it meant to help her escape— everything that I risked, everything that I stood to lose. And that was a lot! The look she gave me still haunts me, as if to imply I was a coward.

Me? A coward?! A hero is more like it. But there was no way of making her understand. She really had lost her mind. From the day she decided to write, the very instant she grabbed the quill and started to scribble. I had tried to stop her. "This is not a ladies' profession, Teresita," I told her. She glared at me, furious, threw the inkwell at me, and maintained an icy silence like I had never felt before. "You idiot!" I said to myself... I don't think I ever understood her. A woman who had everything that a woman longs to have: a wealthy husband, beauty, education, a good home, and a secure future. But no, this woman was a mellifluous spirit, dissolving into her poetry and that of others. She lost herself in the pages of that diary; she showed no one, not even me, all the love she said she felt.

She should be grateful...

TERESA

Yes, it's the train station! My Vicente didn't let me down. I knew he was always organizing my escape. I knew, and that's why I didn't say anything to him. I know how much he loves me. Even though he never admitted it. Poor thing, he'd blush each time I looked at him. My poor Vicente and his wonderful writings. I would've liked to be with him, to leave together, crossing the mountains hand in hand. "Your tickets?" the inspector would say. And he'd open his briefcase and hand over two shiny white tickets to Buenos Aires. Then I'd squeeze his arm even more to feel alive, protected, and loved, and... But wait a minute!

How long was I in the convent? I can't remember; every day was the same as the next, except for the cold and the heat. How many years of cold nights did I endure? How many years of hot days? Could it have been three? Three! Three years! So my daughter must be five, and I must be twenty-four. But hold on! What do I have to thank Vicente for? For coming after three years? And not even accompanying me to the train station! For leaving me to cross the wasteland alone and barefoot? For not thinking of the fresh blood on my ankles or all the stagnant blood I carry within? Not, indeed, for all the copious tears shed for my daughter and him. For him! Because he couldn't confront the "lump" that afternoon. He looked down. He kept quiet. He shrugged his shoulders. He became an accomplice to save himself and his damned writing. It is so much easier to condemn the scatterbrained fool who roams the house humming to herself, the one who scribbles on bits of paper. It's so much easier to do that!

Who are you helping, Vicente? Because you're not helping me. I'm sure you're helping yourself, though. I'm an obstacle for you and your literary career. Of course, what else can it be? The "lump" sends me off to the convent, and you send me to Argentina... The best solution. A crazy recluse with ink-stained fingers is such an inconvenience. This woman who just wants to write poetry bothers you that much...

That's me. But I'm not a package you send to a convent or another country... I am a woman. To hell with Buenos Aires! I'm going back. But not to the convent, no. I'm going to get my daughter. I'm taking her north. I know there are no laws in those parts.

VICENTE

I received a telegram saying that she never arrived. Perhaps she died on the way. At this point, I will never know. I probably should have accompanied her; was it really that risky to stay with Teresa until she got to the train station? But if somebody had seen me, it would have meant my demise as a writer. No, nobody is more valuable than my writing career. Maybe she took the wrong train, or she got off early, not waiting to get to Buenos Aires. Teresa was always unpredictable. You never knew what she was going to do. And that was part of her charm. Oh, Teresa! And where are you now? Did you die on the way? I don't want to think she threw herself on the tracks. My Teresa is so taken with the great romantic novels.

"The heroines always die," you'd complain. You're right. They die or go mad. Or end up in a nunnery.

Teresa, where are you? Don't you dare come back now that everybody looks at me with distrust. Everyone thinks I had something to do with your departure. The editor has frozen my manuscript until "the waters settle," as he said to me while pointing to your picture in the local paper, reporting you lost. How did you manage to appear in the newspaper, Teresita? Especially considering that what your family wanted most was to bury you alive...

TERESA

Carefully and silently. On tiptoes. The dogs know me and won't bark. I'll go to the back of the house, to the servants' entrance. If anybody can help me, it's Rosaura. I always noticed she wasn't that clever. Moving forward on tiptoes. It's my house; I know it well. This is Rosaura's window.

I gently tap on the window pane. I hear noises inside.

Someone peeks through the window. It's Rosaura!

"Señora! You're alive! I knew it; I saw your picture in the paper!"

"Of course I'm alive, Rosaura, but lower your voice..."

"They told us you had died, you know, three years ago." Rosaura says, making the sign of the cross.

"No, I'm more alive than ever. I need to ask you for a favor; there isn't much time. Help me see my daughter. Nothing more, that's all I ask, then I will leave and never come back. I won't tell anybody you helped me."

"That's fine; come in. But don't make any noise," she says with some hesitance.

Rosaura opens the door, and I follow. We carefully walk up the stairs. The creaking wood makes my skin crawl.

"The master isn't here; not to worry. He's gone to Santiago to look for you. He thinks you fled there..." Rosaura says.

There's my daughter's door. I open it slowly. My daughter is taller, almost taking up the whole bed. She is sleeping peacefully. On the nightstand is a photograph of me with a black ribbon. She, too, thinks I've died. I sit by her feet, watch her, and listen to her breathing softly and rhythmically. Her skin is so white and perfect, as is her curly, honey-colored hair. And those eyelashes she got from her grandmother. My baby girl sleeps, and I mustn't wake her up. I make her drink some drops they gave me at the convent, the ones that made me drunk and I wouldn't wake up for days... She barely opens her mouth, swallowing the drops.

VICENTE

I searched for her on the way to the station. I went on foot, tracing the same path she must have followed. Many sharp stones and tree branches were blocking the road. Teresa. Teresa. Now I don't know why I didn't accompany you. I suppose I am a coward. Some branches had torn the habit; there were pieces of fabric still hanging from them. And some red stains are close by. Blood? I prefer to think it wasn't.

Close to the station, I found your habit torn. Did you take it off or did somebody force you? Teresa. Teresa. I should have gone with you.

TERESA - IN WRITING

That night, Rosaura offered me the meager savings she had. I didn't accept, but thanked her for her heartfelt offer. On the other hand, I did take all of my jewelry. With the "lump" in Santiago, I had more than enough time to take a bath, eat and change clothes. Rosaura helped me bandage my ankles and put my boots on. The veiled hat covering my face was perfect. Rosaura's family was able to get a cart to transport me to the train station. We left the house at dawn, my daughter in her old baby carriage, which she barely fit into, sleeping thanks to the "drops" from the convent. No one recognized me, not even in broad daylight. After all, they were looking for a barefoot lunatic wearing a nun's habit who had already been declared dead.

I bought the tickets to board the train that would take me to the *Longitudinal Norte* railway, the famous *Longino* that would get me to Iquique. I paid with a ruby ring; the ticket clerk accepted it because I paid him personally with an emerald one. Two first-class tickets. The inspector helped me with the stroller and my trunk. I moved down the aisle of the coach carefully so my daughter wouldn't wake up, acknowledging the other passengers with a smile and a nod. There weren't many people. When somebody spoke to me, I answered in English, one of my four languages. Thinking I was a foreigner, they left me alone.

I didn't allow my daughter to awaken. When I saw her rousing, I'd give her a few more drops. People soon thought the child was sick, so they kept their distance even more.

When we got to Santiago, we changed trains. We boarded the *Longino*. The faces were different, and there were many English-speaking foreigners. I switched to speaking French so I would be assured a discreet voyage.

The trip lasted three days. By the end of the second day, we started crossing the driest, hottest stretch of land I had ever seen in my life. It was the Atacama desert. Miles and miles of nothing. It was the most despairing part of the journey, worse even than my confinement in the convent or the shoeless walk to the train to Buenos Aires.

After the third day, we reached a town. It was all dust and sand. But it did have a wide street with wooden houses. Iquique. The name had a melodic ring to it. It would be our home.

I got some help at the station to carry my trunk. My daughter was still in her baby carriage and had become quite pale. I was worried because she'd slept the whole way and had barely had some warm milk I gave her from a bottle when she was neither fully awake nor groggy.

The man who assisted me told me about the guest house. He said it was respectable and added, "for fine ladies like you." I asked him to take me there. The house was on Balmaceda street. It was painted light green and had two floors and a balcony. I knocked, and a beautiful brown-skinned woman with freckles opened the door. She greeted me in English, and I answered in German. That was my way of making sure she kept her distance from us. When I showed her the white gold necklace with diamonds, she took my daughter's baby carriage and led me to the room at the far end of the house. It was spacious, with high windows, velvet drapery, and polished wooden floors. There were two rooms. The first was a sitting room with blue upholstered furniture and a Louis XVI replica table. The second bedroom had two beds of forged iron with hand-embroidered bedspreads and a small washbasin and pitcher. A large window offered a view of the ocean. I sat down, exhausted, on the edge of the bed and tried to hold back a ridiculous teardrop.

"Are you all right, Señora?" the woman asked in Spanish. "Yes, everything's fine. Please bring me some fruit," I answered, in Spanish as well, implicitly deciding that this would continue to be our common tongue. "For the girl?"

"Yes…"

"I'll bring some milk as well," she added.

I appreciated her diligence. I closed the door and moved towards the carriage. My daughter was still breathing slowly because of the laudanum. I took her out of the wagon and laid her on the bed. And I began to prepare myself. Because she would see her mother's ghost sitting at the foot of the bed when she started to wake up.

*****

Teresa Wilms Montt, a poet and writer from Chile known for her passionate and avant-garde literary work, served as the inspiration for this story.

14

Marcelita's Amusement

Act I

Marcelita was nineteen years old and a bit beefy, although she was fond of saying "her bones were hiding." When she laughed, two dimples would appear on her cheeks. She knew it was a charming feature, so she practiced smiling in front of the mirror for hours. She had a round belly as if she carried a baby inside, but in fact, she had never even menstruated. Her mother ignored the fact that Marcelita's body was in open rebellion against nature. For her part, Marcelita faked her period with sanitary napkins smeared with blackberry jam.

That was how Marcelita went about in public, with her bulky body, her dry ovaries, and her soap opera smile. She was determined to find a boyfriend who'd want to wed her before she was twenty. She realized she was not a prize attraction in that town of beauties parading around in petite dresses and silver stilettos. Marcelita always clashed with these sleek ostriches, like an elephant shaking its rump as it trampled through the savannah. She felt, nevertheless, that there were an infinite number of reasons beyond being thin that qualified her to be pretty. And there was one more thing as well, Marcelita said: she was intelligent.

With this in mind, when there was barely a month left for her to begin the next chapter of her life, Marcelita got all dolled up to go out one night. She left alone, with her mother's permission. She didn't tell any of her friends, since they all had the bad taste to look her up and down when she wore her black leather miniskirt, her purple bodice top, and a bow jutting out from the crown of her head. No, that night Marcelita would go out by herself because she needed all the space she could get, literally and figuratively, to display her attributes.

The nightclub bouncer knew her well. In fact, after denying her entrance so many times and watching her sad face as she waited outside for her friends to emerge from the dive four hours later, he began to take pity on her. He could see that she was different that night, and he even considered her beautiful.

"Come on in..."

"What?" Marcelita asked in amazement.

"Come on in, but quickly, before they see you..."

"Thank you!" the girl answered, delighted she could go in at last.

The nightclub wasn't what she had imagined. The music was deafening, and there were no water fountains or trapeze artists flying through the air in shiny costumes. There was, however, plenty of it: smoke, sweaty people, women in skimpy dresses, and men with strong, solid arms.

Marcelita was aware that she was being stared at. She stood out. There are two ways about it. But that particular evening, a month before she turned twenty, she didn't really care.

Her eyes panned the room again until she spotted her target: a scrawny guy leaning on the bar. He looked shy and a bit scared. Marcelita thought her voluminous curves would allure this poor, bony creature.

"Hello."

"Hi," the skinny guy answered in a trembling voice. "Do you want to dance?"

"O.K. "

They were heading to the dance floor when Pedro Navaja's *salsa* started. "Perfect!" That was one of Marcelita's favorite songs. She had rehearsed her eyelash flutter and her hip movements to the point of exhaustion with that very song.

The young man wasn't merely skinny, but also shorter than her. Marcelita was nevertheless pleased, as his shortness meant that his face was directly opposite her cleavage.

She grabbed him and pressed him up against her. The scrawny guy was flying, his feet off the ground. Marcelita was able to move her legs with grace, gliding forward, backward, right, and left while yelling, "Turn!" when necessary. This marionette, who was holding her enormous buttocks in both hands, captivated her.

The song ended, and the skinny guy had a difficult time detaching himself from the towering shrew. "Do you want to go somewhere else?" "All right... " the scrawny guy stuttered.

Marcelita had always had a good eye; she was well-trained

from the constant observance of her "hornet" friends as they chose young men to seduce. All those afternoons, they'd pick her up just to make fun of her when they went to the town square to flirt and asked her to sit on the other bench with the pretext that they couldn't all fit on one. All those hours of apprenticeship with her friends ramming their stingers into her were finally paying off.

Marcelita grabbed the skinny guy's arm. She had to stoop a little to avoid the back pain their difference in height caused. They left the nightclub through the main entrance. The guard looked at her, and they winked at each other in complicity. She, too, could pick up a "one-night stud."

Marcelita knew just where to take her bundle of bones. There was a motel around the corner from the club. She was familiar with it because she had had to wait there for the hornets, who asked her to please go along with them, and they were a bit frightened of going in there with a guy they just met. And if she could just sit outside the room on the floor, they'd feel safer. And they were right in their suspicions, because knowing that Marcelita had her ear glued to the door, they'd moan with pleasure even louder. Then they would come out satisfied, their hair all disheveled, thank her, and walk back home together in silence: Marcelita with her six-foot, six-inch frame and the hornets towering along on their *Celia Cruz*-style shoes.

The red light in the reception area indicated there were available rooms. Marcelita rang the bell. The landlady opened the door, looking slightly drowsy. When she saw it was Marcelita playing the lead role in her own sleazy conquest instead of being the constant tag-along, she gave her a smile of approval.

"Room four," the woman indicated as she handed her a roll of toilet paper and a key.

"Thank you," Marcelita answered. The skinny guy remained mute.

The young woman opened the door and, for the first time, could see what was on the other side. It wasn't as she had imagined; there wasn't a four-poster bed or golden drapes hanging from the ceiling. Nor were there any mirrors or a little wash basin with a porcelain pitcher. Quite the contrary: Marcelita saw before her a standard bed with iron posts. There was no blanket or coverlet, just a sheet that had once been white but was now covered with suspicious yellow stains. She assumed that other people had already used this "love nest" that night because the space smelled strongly of sweat.

Marcelita tried to focus on her ultimate goal: finding a husband in less than a month. Getting married before she turned twenty because it was then or never in that tiny town where only the prettiest girls married well. If things didn't work out, she'd have to get a job as a nurse's aide in the local hospital, where she would be obliged to empty chamber pots and wipe the poop from babies' bottoms.

"Do you like it?" Marcelita asked, trying to break the silence.

"It's fine," the guy said.

"Come," she beckoned, grabbing him by the hand and leading him to the bed.

The skinny guy let himself be led, and after a while, he let himself be had as well. Marcelita took off the black T-shirt he was wearing. Then she took off his belt, confirming that her "suitor" had poked a few more notches in it; otherwise, the belt wouldn't have held anything up. Next, she went for the jeans, which were so wide that when she unbuttoned them, the pants fell to the ground. Marcelita ran her eyes over him. His face was neither ugly nor pretty, and his shoulders were narrower than her younger brother's. His legs were bony, with knobby knees that protruded. At half mast, there was a slight rise in his underwear, from which a timid rabbit raised its head. Marcelita didn't want to lose faith. She was already in the middle of her campaign to lose her virginity and provide herself with a husband. So she turned a deaf ear to that inner voice that told her the skinny guy would probably get lost inside of her, and she'd end up in the hospital cleaning up pee and poop, only this time with a nurse trying to dive into her to find him.

"Down to business," she said to herself. She decided to lie face-up on the bed, which she confirmed was almost too small for her. She grabbed the scrawny guy by the arm and planted him on top of her.

"Go for it. Put it in."

"Right now?"

"Yes. Right now... "

The skinny guy obeyed. Thank goodness he had no mind of his own. Mounted on top of the Everest that was Marcelita, the poor guy did all he could to find the opening between the tight folds surrounding her crotch. As things progressed, he got quite excited as well. The little rabbit became a hare, although for Marcelita, it was no more than a warm, moist pinky finger trying to penetrate her.

"Done... " the guy sighed.

His performance was over, of course. And he was exhausted. He dismounted the round body and tried to settle in a corner of the bed. As he didn't fit, he chose to place himself across the foot of the bed. He took a cigarette out of his pants pocket and lit it.

For Marcelita, that gesture was akin to total consummation.

She sat up with difficulty, feeling the bedsprings poking into her hips a bit. This actually made her happy because she had so much padding in that area that she didn't usually feel anything, not even when she sat on the knitting needles that her mother always left on the sofa. She wiped herself with the toilet paper and struggled to get dressed, the leather skirt sticking to her sweat-soaked skin.

"Ready, then," she said. "Let's get out of here."

The skinny guy was surprised. He had thought they'd stay there for a while.

"Oh. All right," he answered again with the same lack of resolve he had shown during the entire improvised date.

They left the room, and Marcelita locked the door. As they advanced through the hallway, they could hear far more moans of pleasure than she had been able to fake.

Near the front door, the landlady was asleep in an armchair. The television was still on. Marcelita dropped the key in a mussel shell the woman had left for that purpose on a little table.

Once outside, the skinny guy had no idea what to say.

But Marcelita did.

"Come and see me tomorrow. Here's my address," Marcelita

said, handing him a slip of paper that she already had prepared before leaving home.

"What time?"

"Six p.m."

"O.K. Bye."

"Bye," she answered, and she bent down to give him the only kiss proffered that night.

The next day, Marcelita was nervous but cheerful. It was five minutes to six when the doorbell rang. She went running to the door and found the skinny guy standing there, with his hair slicked back, wearing a white T-shirt and a leather jacket. It seemed he had taken pains to make a good impression.

Marcelita brought him in and sat him on her mother's sofa. The knitting needles poked at the skinny guy. Marcelita removed them and told him to wait there.

The living room was modest: there was the famous sofa, two wooden chairs, and a dining table that seated four. The walls were "upholstered" with images of Jesus, some dying, some resurrecting, and not many smiling. On the biggest wall was a portrait of Our Lady of Guadalupe. Next to the television, which crowned the room, was a little statue of Our Lady of Mount Carmel. The tick-tock of the wall clock kept time with the pace of the young man's breathing, who suddenly felt uneasy.

"What! That's impossible! I'll kill him!"

A furious roar arose from the kitchen: plates crashing to the floor, glass breaking, and the sound of what seemed to be a fist pounding on a table were heard.

The skinny guy jumped up from the sofa, scared and ready

to run off, but his weak character kept him from actually moving.

Later, you could hear mumbling and weeping, then there was a long silence and hurried steps from the kitchen to the living room.

"You're the one, you miserable wretch! I'll kill you!"

It was Marcelita's father, red-faced with fury after discovering his daughter had been deflowered the night before. Marcelita and her mother followed him into the living room.

"No! Antonio! Leave him alone! We have to find another way to settle this," answered her mother, in tears.

"*What* other way?!" her father shouted again.

With all the commotion, the neighbors had already crowded together in front of the windows to find out what was happening.

"We can get married." Marcelita said it in a whisper. "Get married! Get married! Get married!" The more her father said it, the more it started to make sense.

It was a small town, and the gossipy neighbors had already found out everything—the daughter's honor had been compromised.

"Get married! Yes, that's what you'll have to do," added her father in a spirit of conciliation, convinced it was the only way to salvage the situation.

Marcelita smiled, pleased at the result. The skinny guy was even paler than usual and stood there speechless.

"But... " he dared to say.

"But *what* ?" her father shot back, walking towards him with clenched fists. He was two heads taller than the skinny guy. "Uh, no, I just wanted to know when..." the skinny guy said, seeing himself so defenseless against the colossal man threatening to strike him.

All things considered, the better option was to marry her rather than risk her father strangling him.

And thus, the case was closed. Two weeks later, Marcelita announced she was pregnant. Her mother no longer had to buy extra jars of blackberry jam, as she used to do every month without really knowing why.

The strictly private wedding took place at the church. Only Marcelita's family attended and a couple of the skinny guy's friends. The skinny guy, it turned out, was a conscript who hadn't been able to shake off his mandatory military service, even though he was utterly scrawny and not fit for a battle zone of any description. He had been stationed in town with his battalion for three months, and while all his friends were having fun with the local hornets, he hadn't shared the same luck. In the final analysis, Marcelita's interest in him, the day they met— it all really suited him to a tee.

As his family from the south was unable to travel all those miles to the northern region of the country, they had to be content with sending him a telegram on the big day, congratulating the skinny guy and "the bride, who must be beautiful."

Marcelita wore a white veil, even though her mother had begged her not to do so. But she wanted a "proper" wedding with all the pomp and circumstance. And thus she made her appearance immaculate, smiling, and happy, satisfied with being the first girl in her circle of friends to get married before turning twenty. With that, she had managed to escape a destiny of smelly bedpans as well as settle the score for all the years of mockery and humiliation to which her friends had subjected her. "All put to the best use," she said, at last, polishing her gold wedding ring with her white veil.

Act II

Dear diary:

Nine months have passed, but nobody has a clue that the extra rolls of fat aren't the baby, but rather the doughnuts my mom makes on the weekends. I like being pregnant, even if it's fake, because they take me out, they let me eat all the chocolates I want, and nobody bothers me anymore if they see me lying on the bed or sofa all day. Things are going well. Alejandro, my husband, is rather dim-witted and quiet. He doesn't ask questions. He's content with being on top of me once a week.

That's good for both of us because now that I'm married, I don't have to work at the hospital. My mom always told me it was my only hope, that with the sugar-coated brain I had, I wasn't fit to do anything else. I've never had a perfect sense of smell, and I wouldn't have been able to stand the stench of the hospital. People say I was born "sweet" and thus spent many months inside a machine that looked like an oven, with a bright light that nearly left me blind, without any clothes, and close to a round window through which my mother could put her hand. It's not that I'm dumb, my mother says. It's just that I'm less intelligent. But that's more than enough for me: I already have a husband, and I have saved myself from the fate of working at the hospital.

This child already has a name: it is René. And people send us gifts to fill his clothes chest. Many packages have arrived from the south of Chile and contain hand-woven blankets of coarse wool that smell of sheep. Alejandro says his grandmother is an artisan and can't see, but her hands haven't forgotten how to knit a shawl. A little pink dress has also arrived. His grandmother believes she is psychic and has sworn that the imaginary baby will be a girl.

All of this makes me laugh, but to be honest, sometimes I feel the guilt creeping in. I don't want to think about it, not even about what I'll do when the last day of these nine months arrives, when they've treated me like a queen, only to find out that the sweets were just for me, not for the baby. The guilt is worse when my mother comes and touches my belly, puts her left ear on me, and tries to guess the child's first words. The flatulence produced from eating broccoli is useful. My mom crosses herself when she hears a hissing sound, which is no more than gas passing through my gut.

I had a sharp eye when I chose Alejandro. I needed a thick-headed man like him. None of this would have worked with any other man. And with that said, I have to confess that marriage isn't what I had imagined... He spends the week with his regiment and arrives here on Saturday afternoon. He returns on Sunday morning. He gives me all the money they pay him. It's a pittance, really, but it's enough to pay for mangos, nail polish, and depilatory creams. And hair dye, of course. Since becoming pregnant, I've gone blonde.

The other day, my mother brought me a book from the library on childbirth. I looked at all the pictures, and I even read some of it, particularly the chapters about labor pains. I needed to know what sort of face to make when I am supposedly giving birth. What does it mean to lose a baby then, even if I can persuade them that it fell before I could get a hold of it?

Act III

Marcelita gained so much weight that she achieved something somewhat unique: stretching her skin to the point of transparency so that you could see her internal organs. But she was still flirty, with the dimples on her cheeks, and with the fake pregnancy, even her breasts had grown into volcanoes, like San Pedro and San Pablo, towering and majestic. Marcelita was happy. The master plan had been followed to perfection.

Without her knowing, her mother had asked the local midwife to assist her at a reduced price. Of all the doughnuts her mother baked each weekend, half were for Marcelita, and the other half were for sale in the town square. Also, Alejandro had to pass by his mother-in-law's kitchen on each of his Saturday visits before seeing Marcelita. His mother-in-law forced him to hand over two-thirds of the money the army paid him so she could add it to her savings fund, which was destined to guarantee a safe delivery for Marcelita. Her mother was frightened at the prospect of Marcelita's baby sharing the same fate as her daughter when she was born: being huge, getting trapped in the birth canal, and losing precious oxygen to the brain. Her mother was right: Marcelita wasn't dim-witted, just slow. But what she couldn't show off with intelligence, she made up for with her unique fancies. She could find the most unexpected ways to get what she wanted. She had always been like that, even when she convinced them not to send her to school anymore because she wanted to devote herself to cleaning children in the hospital pediatric ward.

And so, the last day of Marcelita's nine months arrived. She'd never been organized, but she did buy a calendar with white kittens, which announced the passing of time. On the day in question, Marcelita practiced in front of the bathroom, mirroring the grimaces of pain that would accompany her imaginary labor. First, she'd furrow her eyebrows, then squeeze her eyes so tight that her nose would turn red. After that, she'd open her mouth wide and keep it like that, holding her breath as long as she could. She'd inhale loud shrieks while arching her back and holding her belly with both hands. Convinced that her act was believable, she went to the living room and prepared to give birth.

She sat on her armchair, and the show began. She thought she was decent, and as soon as she finished with the fake birth, she'd try to become an actress. Suddenly, she started to feel a pain so fierce that it split her hips in half. She wasn't able to straighten up anymore. She clung to her belly, which got stiff as a stone every three minutes. Her last scream came out so strong that she ended up attracting all the family's attention, who came running to the room. Marcelita observed with horror that she had peed on the armchair. Her bright-pink pompom slippers were ruined forever. She cried—for the slippers, of course. No imaginary child had the right to damage her possessions. When her mother saw her, she sat by her side, touched her belly, and calculated that it was stiffening every sixty seconds.

"It's time!" she screamed at her father, who took a small suitcase decorated with big-eared chimpanzees out of the closet. "Come on, girl!" Marcelita's father shouted at her, trying to lift that body twisted in contractions. And fat— so very fat.

Outside, her mother was already waiting with a taxi. They put her in the back seat as best they could and squeezed themselves in around the layers of tulle in Marcelita's skirt.

"What's happening?" Marcelita yelled, already scared by now. The theatrics were almost too real.

Her mother responded, a little suffocated due to the lack of air in that small space, "You're in labor, my girl!"

"But I can't be! I'm not pregnant!"

Her parents fell silent. Marcelita tended to fantasize, and now the main theme of her new movie was to deny the pregnancy.

They arrived at the hospital in a few minutes. Her mother's friend, the midwife, was waiting at the door with a stretcher.

"How long ago did she go into labor?" the woman dressed in white asked.

"About half an hour ago..." her mother answered.

"She's almost there, then," the midwife commented, looking at Marcelita's distorted face.And she was right.

Marcelita was like a submarine, shooting torpedoes. In the delivery room, her nose itched, she sneezed, and the baby flew out like a polished bullet. Luckily, the midwife was on alert and caught it in mid-air.

It was a girl. The grandmother from the south was right. Renata cried so sharply that Marcelita's parents heard it outside in the waiting room. Furthermore, Marcelita remained stunned, still convinced that this sticky bundle couldn't have come from her loins.

"What is *that* ?" "Your baby, a girl... "

"It can't be! It's all a lie! I wasn't pregnant; I made it all up."

"What did you think, Marcela?" the midwife asked her very seriously, in response to Marcelita's insistence. "That you could fake a pregnancy?"

"Yes," Marcelita answered dryly, thinking that childbirth, in the end, wasn't as she had imagined it.

Her baby girl didn't have a pink ribbon around the single curl on her head, nor did she wear cotton pants. There were no angelical choirs to accompany the feat either.

It was then that she thought she must devise a way to rid herself of Renata. But not just yet; she felt exhausted and wanted to enjoy the presents they would give her.

"There's still plenty of time for that," she said to herself. "Plenty of time for that."

* * * * *

San Pedro and San Pablo are two neighboring volcanoes in the Antofagasta region; they are more than 19.000 miles high.

15

Añañuca - Chachacoma

Part I - Añañuca

How do I wrench the ancestral rage, lodged between my hips, from the thousands of rose-colored paths laid out for me? What to do with the body that bends over, gets up, keeps warm, becomes cold, and awakens feelings of desire and hate at the same time? And perhaps whose rhythm, secret, or even the moon controls the moist dance between my legs.

How do you mend the soul that has been broken for so long? Broken by a silent wound that never took shape in anyone's mouth, it was never spoken in any language and was cloaked from birth in other sounds to silence it—a tear shed by no one.

What did my mother do? Who *is* my mother? I want to know, and yet I don't, rather like the compelling ritual of incessantly licking a lip wound, which won't heal because it's being licked incessantly.

Like forever scratching a mosquito bite, like putting lemon on it and continuing to scrub over it with the dried-up lemon, the blackish-red skin turned raw by the itch.

The burning sensation.

The soul is broken. It rises and demands a response. The broken soul pummels the abdomen and dries up the blood and all its tributaries. Grief explodes in the lower belly.

It comes out of the eyes as well, wide open, and turns itself into a shriveled desert tree. From the neck to the waist.

No feeling in the legs. Everything is numb until touched by his caress, this casual boyfriend I need, so I can respond to the invitation of his ardent rhythms but also to reject the dominance of others one more time. So, I can do what I want, not what they ask me to do.

To seek further to awaken that part of me destroyed so many years ago that I don't even know how many. To take my feelings beyond my mother's breast mark. Exhale. A birth-mark runs along my forearm, climbs my shoulder, and goes down again, finishing up at the center of my chest. Thousands of planets are dancing inside me. A blemish nobody in my fair-haired family possesses. Was I burned as a child? They had to safeguard their possession of this body, which has always wanted to escape. I have a "stained" arm, brown hair, and blackish cheeks. I have nothing of theirs, and yet they have me.

From the frown on my forehead to the numb legs to the casual boyfriend.

To the continuous feeling of expelling.

To the continuous sensation of menstruating. Which doesn't come.

I come from other times with other customs. I sense that they brought me, by force, to this dampness that gets trapped in my throat. And inflames me. Pus. Pestilence. I know I am another person, that there is a different landscape within me. I inherited a birthmark from someone I don't know. Where am I going? Where have I been? I carry a head on my shoulders that thinks differently, a round weight that questions everything. I look around me and wish for what is common, normal, calm, and warm. But my body is anxious for liberation.

Where can I seek that space where I am only me? Without a long last name, without green velvet dresses that do not go well with my dark coloring? Where do I come from? Green velvet in the Atacama Desert.

I know someone preserves the scriptures of my departure. Somebody has taken note of all my steps that went astray. A small heavenly notebook where the gods have written who I was later tossed into the rubbish. Because Inti tells me more than the bearded man who hangs and bleeds in the church. The beams of light from Indi tell me that I belong to other climes: thinner, sharper, and rougher. Because my skin is different, my hips are not the same.

I've lost something.

Or someone has lost me.

Part II - Chachacoma

Twelve or thirteen. I don't remember. In those days, they used to call me Visvira. My head anchored in thick chain-link braids.

Straight black hair. My grandmother wove it to give it a bit of shape, so the waves would hide my Indian profile. *Your father's face*, she always said.

On the first morning of winter one year, Surire gave her a bundle of herbs to soak my hair in.

By twelve or thirteen, my hair began to grow lighter. To dry up slowly. To turn into withered grass.

Grandmother was perfectly content with my translucent strands, scores of them lying lifeless on my head by sunrise each day. It didn't bother her that my bristly hair looked like a wild pasture.

From thirteen to fifteen or sixteen, I became acquainted with the local sheriff.

Through the faded horizon of the Andean *altiplano*, this horseman would announce his first and soon-to-be frequent visits with spirals of dust etched against an azure sky.

My figure soon became a prodigious weapon. A subtle twist of the hips would tame the sheriff, who responded with gifts of fresh cheese or alpaca yarn.

"Flor de la Puna" he called me, balancing on burning knees under an opening in the mud wall that served as a window. Just a brief glimpse of a moon-kissed shoulder was enough to cause him to explode, becoming more submissive.

Very few nights went by before he took me away. He came

with two sheep tied by the neck and a llama adorned with colorful garlands.

Grandmother took the rope that held the animals and placed my arm on the sheriff's hand. Words weren't needed; nothing was said.

We went even higher up. The sharp blades of the mountain wind scraped my nose.

Dark petals of *puna* covered my face, creating a sandy layer that protected my skin.

My belly is growing round. But I was also alone. No longer *Visvira*, I was now to be called *Chachacoma*. He had left three months earlier, looking for new business. It had been two years since he was supposed to return.

I gave birth during the wait. It was a girl, with grey eyes and her left arm covered in moles, going up her shoulder and culminating on her chest. The firmament was confined to her forearm, just like mine.

A rough autumn. The crops were sealed over due to the frosts. My breasts denied nourishment to the baby girl, who chewed on her hunger, cheated by the nipple's warm breath.

When the last leaf had fallen on the plantation, another sheriff came and took her away. Wrapped in blankets, resting on someone's back, I watched her leave.

"In the city, she'll have food," he said. "Don't be concerned. She'll be all right. She'll come back in the spring."

I kept staring at the mountains, the unfulfilled promise

of the fruit wrapped in seed, and the narrow path to Uyuni emerging brightly at sunset.

The path my husband took led to the other side of the mountains.

I yearned to see his tiny figure moving along that trail, past mountain crags, back to his wife and daughter's side while carrying his bag across his chest.

I pictured him during the afternoons until my eyes could not distinguish rock from goat.

In a matter of minutes, hours, twenty, or forty years later, they brought me here.

This time without a dowry, without *chachacoma* flower buds, alone in the back of a wagon belonging to the people who bought the last harvest my land had to offer and to whom I signed over the documents that prevented me from ever returning.

I eventually arrived in this wasteland of twisted bodies and crooked smiles, hiding a lack of teeth. Of pain, rashes, and the vinegary odor of wrinkles.

It was here that I found out my daughter was alive because of the unique birthmarks on her arm. She had come to say goodbye to the oldest resident, who was dying of liver disease.

He had served an old family, which, when told about his malady, made arrangements to abandon him in this refuge.

On that night, some of the house stewards and servants came to say goodbye.

Then I saw her come in, upright and floating, wearing multi-colored skirts. She slowly approached the dying man's bed.

She took his hand and began to sing to him softly, in

languages unknown to me. She didn't stay long, perhaps a few minutes.

I bumped into her by the door, where I had been waiting. I spoke to her. She smiled and shrugged her shoulders. She didn't understand a thing.

Then I remembered that I hadn't had time, when she was a child, to teach her my tongue.

During all the nights in which I drew stars across the sky of my empty void, I never thought I'd see her again. And yet, there, in that place that reeked of sourness, I had come across my daughter.

The deception still hurts in my gut. She was going to return in the spring, but she didn't.

I watched every hawthorn bloom and every *tamarugo* flower wither without her coming back.

I began to wither myself.

The other sheriff hadn't kept his word. He had taken her away forever. And I, tied to the harsh lands of the *altiplano*, did not abandon that orchard, which was slowly and silently dying.

In this place permeated with urine and the stammering of the old and diseased, I have found her again. Ever since the first night I saw her, she has come back every day to visit the dying man.

I get ready in rags and comb my hair, which is still brittle from the harsh herbal treatments I received as a child.

My daughter, with her coarse hair, appears. She moves forward as if she had no feet; she seems to fly. Skirts shine brightly as we ourselves begin to grow dark.

This time, I plant myself squarely in front of her. She will not leave without hearing her story. She looks at me with a gaze that goes back to the dawn of time.

"I am your mother," I tell her. Again, she ignores me.

I follow her, advancing stealthily from behind, like lizards entering their lair. "It's me," I repeat as I grab her arm.

She turns away annoyed, harboring an earthly rage not to be found higher up in the simple air of the *altiplano*.

I have no choice but to show her my forearm. The spots are revealed for her to see. The same kind, color, and size. An identical cosmos has imprinted both of our beings.

Those spots that grandmother wanted to erase, thinking they had deliberately left out a head of cattle in the exchange with the sheriff because of them.

Those spots are the answers to questions asked at other times and on other planes.

My daughter looks at her arm. She touches my spots as if I were trying to read them. Or conjure something up. She scratches her arm as if she wants it to bleed.

She leaves. I see her depart once again. I understand now that we cannot be together. Inti has written separate chapters for us. I began to cry.

But she stops halfway through her escape. And she turns around, her eyes filled with tears. She takes my arm and compares our markings. Identical. She remains motionless for seconds that last for centuries.

Then she points to some chairs in the courtyard of the hospice. She wants us to talk.

Still too many words to string together. And harvests to

reap. And seeds to plant. Voids to fill. But now we have time. She has understood.

"Añañuca," I call her for the first time.

She smiles at me, her eyes shining. She tries, but is unable to repeat her name.

* * * * *

Añañuca: a native flower to Chile, is a vibrant, trumpet-shaped bloom found in arid regions, known for its striking red or yellow colors.

Chachacoma: a flower native to the Andean highlands, is a medicinal plant with small yellow blooms, traditionally used to alleviate altitude sickness.

Tamarugo: The Tamarugo tree is a drought-resistant species native to northern Chile's Atacama Desert, thriving in extreme conditions with deep roots accessing underground water.

Altiplano: a high plateau region located on the skirts of the Andes mountain range.

Flor de la Puna: a small medicinal flower growing in

the Antofagasta and Atacama regions of Northern Chile, at around 11.000 meters above sea level, is used to treat mountain (altitude) sickness.

About The Author

Andrea Amosson (Chile, 1973) is a Chilean journalist and author who lives in Texas, USA, with her husband and two children.

She is the author of four historical fiction novels, one contemporary fiction novel, and two collections of short stories.

Her texts have been published in Chile, Spain, Peru, Colombia, and the USA.

She is a two-time winner of the Gold Medal in the International Latino Book Awards, Rudy Anaya Best Latino Fiction Book, in 2017 and 2022.

Andrea Amosson has taught creative writing in Spanish since 2013 in the Dallas, Texas, area.

Printed in the USA
CPSIA information can be obtained
at www.ICGtesting.com
LVHW060602080724
784630LV00005B/11